TRIBE OF LEGEND

BOOK 1—THE AWAKENING

Markee Drummer

Fulton Books, Inc.
Meadville, PA

Published by Fulton Books 2020

ISBN 978-1-64654-893-4 (paperback)
ISBN 978-1-64654-894-1 (digital)

Printed in the United States of America

CHAPTER 1

PROCEEDING IN THE FOURTH QUARTER with thirty-six seconds remaining on the clock, down by five points in Florida's high school state semifinals basketball game, the Providencia Beach Raiders are now in possession of the ball. At the free-throw line with an opportunity to put the points of the Raiders' team closer to tying or taking the lead, Ronin Drummond, Raiders' junior player, with palms sweaty and heartbeat racing, is thinking to himself, *Breathe, relax. These are just free throws. I have shot a million of these—five in the morning, lights out in the gym, outside in thirty-degree windchills while it is raining cats and dogs. Therefore, I have trained so hard for moments like these.* Ronin then takes one last deep inhale of air and then exhales. With one bounce of the basketball, then a spin of the spherical object in his hand like a globe turning on its axis, the Raiders' player bends his knees, feet rooted to the court, then rises in one fluid motion, and releases the ball from his hands. *Swish!*

Attempt number 1 is good, and with it, comes an enthusiastic holler from the crowd of about two thousand excited high school basketball fans.

Coach Frank Beasley, with a look anxiety from the far reaches of the universe, shouts, "Ronin, you got this!"

Ronin, who's at the free-throw line, preparing to make an attempt at shot number 2, catches a voice in his head like a whisper: "Ronin, greatness lies deep within you, astonishing potential, a bloodline of champions, a bloodline of kings!"

"Let's go!" A pat on Ronin's butt comes from Raiders teammate and best friend, Paul "PG" Griggs, as he mutters in the ear of his startled comrade, "Yeah, you got this in the bag!"

Suddenly, he has a flashback:

> "Come on, PG, let's get it. I won't stop. You won't stop. I got you if you die out here. You got me if I die out here! We are in the trenches!" It's a vivid vision of Ronin and Paul in what looks like an intensive workout session, including a combination of various stretches, wind sprints, ball-handling drills, layups, and jump shots.
>
> "How can we fail if we never give up?" asks Ronin.
>
> "Well, if our legs give out, you can carry me" comes from Paul, then a winded laugh comes from both of the young men proceeding to their routine.

With one dribble of the basketball, then into a spin within his hand, Ronin bends at the knee and rises, and in one fluid motion, the ball rolls off the tip of his fingers, and with a bank off the backboard and a chilling lean off the rim into a cyclone motion as if a toilet bowl flushing down it's vortex, in goes shot attempt number 2. An enormous roar of excitement and anticipation from the Raiders' faithful erupts.

"Defense! Defense! Defense!" chants the fans.

A blown whistle from the referee alerts both competing teams that the basketball is now being put back into playing action and then passes the ball to Daniel "Danny Boy" Rudolph, starting shooting guard and small forward for the opposing Eagles of St. Petersburgh High School. On the previous season as a junior, Rudolph earned himself the title of State Player of the Year. Rudolph, pursuing the title a second time in a row, also has ideas of celebrating this year with a bonus gift of a state championship in mind, but his rival is on a mission to spoil the plans of the state's best.

"Time-out! Time-out! Time-out!" bellows Coach Beasley from the bench of the Raiders in the direction of the nearest referee. Ronin and Paul are jogging with fellow teammates toward their coach to form a huddle.

"Time for Beasley to coach us up. We need to take advantage of this momentum," says Paul.

"Yeah, we most definitely needed that swing, especially after being down by twenty-five points at the half," answers Ronin.

"Fellas, fellas!"—anxious faces encircled in the huddle—"I called this time-out to calm you down a little bit," explains Coach Beasley, soaked in his body's moisture as if he had been standing in South Florida during the summertime at high noon waiting at a bus stop in a three-piece suit. His voice is raspy and nearly gone from the stress of being overworked. "We have been running our 1-3-1 trap defense and doing a heck of a job in the second half executing, but now down in time at crunch time. We are going to need to amp it up on this last push and close the game out, playing our full-court press defense. We need to get a steal. We must have the ball now, so let's go and get it. One more thing, no matter the results tonight, I just want you guys to know that I am proud of you and love you guys! Thirty-six seconds left, guys, until that fat lady comes on stage and steals the spotlight. Come on, guys, bring it in. Your moment is right now!"

Fifteen pairs of hands formed as fists are placed together, and the whole team shouts, "One, two, three, go, Raiders!"

*****

The basketball is now back in play. Ronin is now positioned, ready in his defensive stance—hands up and swinging wildly in attempts to be as disruptive and annoying as possible. The faces of Ronin and Danny Boy are engaged in a small contest of a stare-down. In the minds of the two competitors is this: challenge assigned, and challenge accepted.

Danny Boy tosses the ball into his team's point guard and gives Ronin a good shove of his elbow to the ribcage of the Raider, unnoticed by the referee, as he sprints past inbounds in his attempt to cut the defender off his path on his mission to trap the basketball in its proper location. As soon as the ball handler reaches across the half-court line, if timed and executed properly, the ball handler should become trapped in a swarm of scrappy and screaming hands getting after the ball, forcing the handler to pick up the ball. Pressured into a situation with no dribbles, the Eagles point guard apprehensively needs to get the ball out of his hands, like a game of hot potato. Ronin pays little attention to the elbow and bump from his opponent. Thus far, he keeps his focus on his mark, pacing where he feels the ball handler is attempting to go and not where he is positioned now, beating him to the spot before he can get there. It could not have been a movie shot in one perfect cut; Ronin gains a perfect location just in the nick of time as the Eagles' ball handler crosses the half-court line, which is defended by a pestering Raiders small forward, Tim Jackson, distracting the Eagles' handler from paying any attention to his right side to notice the blind spot that has been created. The Eagles' point guard collects his dribble in an attempt to locate a running mate. Needing to get the ball out of his possession, he turns on his pivot foot and catches a glance of Danny Boy from his peripheral vision racing to the aid of his comrade; he then flings the ball in the direction of Danny Boy. On its course out of the Eagles' offensive player's hand, the ball is tipped by the fingers of Tim, and like a peregrine falcon swooping in to pilfer a catch, Ronin dashes in front of Danny Boy. He's now taking on control of the deflected ball.

The turn of events leads Tim Jackson into an immediate gallop toward the Raiders' basketball hoop, Ronin quarterbacking a Donovan McNabb-type pass without a second's reaction, connecting with his intended target resulting in a freakishly athletic dunk from Tim Jackson that elicited an electrified cheer of joy from the number of Raiders' fans! The mass of spectators are on the edge of their seats or standing eagerly at attention now that the contest is a one-point game with only twenty-five seconds remaining in regulation. A time-out call comes from the opposing Eagles' coach now to gather his team and determine their next plan of attack.

The Raiders are gathered in their collective huddle, deciding on a counterattack, with Coach Beasley at the lead.

"That worked well last out on defense, so we won't fix what's not broken and run the same play. But we must be careful because of our foul situation. Play tough yet cautious. We do not need to give away any more freebies. Everybody, in 1, 2, 3, go, Raiders!"

With the ball back in play, the Eagles' coach, of course, now has switched his offensive strategy to highlight the decision-making skills and athletic attributes of his best player—Danny Boy. With it being such a crucial stretch in the contest, it is the most logical choice. James Cameron, Eagles' forward, now "inbounding" the basketball, hurls the ball in the direction of a blazing Danny Boy, who is coming toward the ball like a locomotive demanding to take control of the ball. Raiders' senior point guard, Erik Akins, trails the guard in his best efforts to keep pace with the state's best player to continue playing smothering defense, according to the plan of trapping the basketball when it crosses the half-court line. Ronin is in hot pursuit, following the flow of the ball; simultaneously, his other teammates take their positions, ready to pounce at any opportunity Danny Boy mishandles the basketball.

Ronin is currently approaching Danny Boy's location as he maneuvers closer to the half-court line. Being in a similar position as his teammate on the previous play, Ronin is anxious to meet his teammate Erik and Danny Boy at the rendezvous point. But unlike the previous player, Danny Boy has another plan in mind. Instead of picking up his dribble and looking for a teammate to bail him out and as Ronin and Erik come to the point of setting their feet in unity to make a successful trap, Danny Boy—a true master of his craft, poised—like poetry in motion, hits another gear with the speed of his dribble and goes from somewhat of a sprint to a sudden stop and stutter step with the ball, causing Erik to shift his weight in an awkward manner putting him in a slight lean to the right side of his body. In the same instance, Danny Boy drops the basketball behind his back with his left hand and, like toying with a yo-yo on a string, brings the ball up in his right hand, stepping through and splitting right between the two Raiders defenders. Knowing the costly stagger in position, the next Raiders player is up and in ready position for the 2-2-1 trap defense, as their mates give chase to reposition themselves.

"Short corner, short corner!" yells Danny Boy, moving with the basketball like a ballerina around the next two defenders. He bounces the ball between his legs and then zips the ball across the court to the opposite corner and finds his positioned teammate who's seeking to make his way to the hoop and driving the baseline.

Melvin "Big Dee" Davis—Raiders' center, standing at an imposing six feet eight inches in height at the age of fifteen—defends his post and blocks the Eagles player, sealing off the open lane to the basket.

Danny Boy—constantly moving without the basketball, displaying great stamina and high basketball IQ—cuts quickly across the face of a winded defender in Erik, taking advantage of his quick first step. Danny Boy takes a direct path down the middle of the lane while flashing his hands, makes himself available to receive a bounce pass delivered by an Eagles mate who is smothered by Big Dee, and then goes up for a layup. Basket's good!

Seven seconds remaining on the clock, the Raiders, down by three points, eagerly look to their leader and coach for guidance, who is now communicating through sign language, being that he used the team's remaining time-out at the thirty-six-second mark.

Senior guard Matt Bowers connects eyes with Coach Beasley, recognizing the fist and palm placed together, symbolizing which play to run. "Power, power, power!" commands Matt, trying to take control of the tempo of the game and maximize his ball usage, having only seven seconds on the clock.

Buzz!

"Foul!" howls the referee.

Matt takes a whack from a careless Eagles defender. Two seconds off the clock, the basketball is now being inbounded at half-court. Being the Eagles' sixth foul of the half, they had a foul to give before putting the Raiders at the free-throw line for bonus shots. It did allow for the Raiders to take advantage of inching closer to the basket, not having to run anytime off the clock.

The gymnasium is filled, standing-room only, but is so quiet at this moment you could hear a pin drop. Ronin is caught deep in a gaze of concentration, oblivious to the noise and numb to the crowd, like the feeling of being inside a tunnel of rushing winds.

A voice speaks to Ronin, "Steel your emotions, greatness runs deep within you."

A distant blare from the whistle being blown snaps Ronin back into ready mode. With the ball back in motion, Ronin takes his position to set a screen on the Eagles player who's defending the guard Erik. Matt tosses the basketball inbounds to Erik who's coming off the screen set by Ronin, then himself going into a roll toward the basket, ready to assist his teammate. By rolling to the basket after the screen, Ronin forces the Eagles defending the hoop to make a choice—either he steps up and helps contest Erik, leaving Ronin free to catch a good quality pass; or he can stay in place, guarding Ronin and allowing Erik to take advantage of the open lane. The Eagles defender makes a jab step in the direction of Erik, just slightly giving his top effort in distracting the basketball handler and staying on his man; he quickly returns to his original position of guarding Ronin. With Erik's eyes widening at the gesture, he proceeds to cross over— left hand to right hand—dribble, dribble, and then up into the lane for the layup.

Ronin, focusing on the rotation of the ball and its bounce as it leaves the palm of Erik, puts his body in between the Eagles defender and drops into a squatting stance called a "box out." This move is used to help players get an edge on rebounding a missed shot. Off the rim, the ball ricochets, and in the same instant, Ronin explodes to a powerful vertical leap snatching the basketball in midair afterward twisting his body in the air as if he were levitating. Ronin spots the Raiders' best shooter and offensive player, Michael Gee, isolated at the elbow of the three-point line. As his defender slacks off his area in help position, Michael excitedly throws his hands. While all defenders are scrambling to locate their offensive opponents, Ronin launches the ball at the hands of the ready shooter. Two seconds on the clock, hardly meeting the hands of Michael, he shoots the ball, and the fans takes a deep inhale, watching in awe and suspense.

It seems as if a lifetime is going by as the basketball traveled on its path to the basket, seeking a perfect landing and connecting through the hoop, like a rainbow linking to a pot of gold at the end of it.

Bing! The clang of the rim echoes through the gym as the ball hits it's front side, falling short of the net and into the palms of an Eagles player.

Buzzz! The ring comes from the buzzer signifying that the contest has ended. The Eagles' rebounder tosses the basketball up into the air with a victorious yell of triumph.

The Eagles' horde is now stampeding out of the stands onto the court in celebration, chanting "Let's go, Eagles! Let's go!" The Eagles team is blissfully advancing on to the state championship game while the Raiders are devastated from the season-ending loss. In an effort to display good sportsmanship, both teams gather in two lines to begin the regulatory end-of-the-game handshake.

"Good game! Good game! Good game!" The players and coaches salute to one another as the competitors stroll past each other, the Raiders squad exhibiting a dejected gaze from the results of the game. Ronin is brooding to himself as the team makes their way to the visitors' locker room to hear Coach Beasley's end-of-the-game remarks and shower up for the ride home.

"We were too careless with the ball early in the game. We played right into their tempo in the first quarter, which lead to seven first-half turnovers, possessions lost by the Raiders that aided in the Eagles being up by twenty-five points at halftime. Fourteen points off fast breaks, Danny Boy connects on all three of his three point attempts during the second quarter, plus two foul shots. We got ourselves settled and, together in the second half, pushed a good run but, it was too little, too late. We fell short." As he enters through the doors of the locker room, he speaks to himself under his breath, "Almost does not count, homey!"

Sobs of sadness are coming from the senior players. The thought of this being their last basketball game in high school or maybe the last sporting competition in their lives, they contemplate over the things they could have done more or less of while out on the hardwood. The group of players, currently sitting in the locker room, silently waits for their coach's address. Coach Beasley enters the room, commanding the attention of the defeated bunch.

"Guys, I just want to start out by saying, I know we did not come here for moral victory and encouraging words at the end of this journey. We came here on a mission to take the whole thing. We knew at the beginning of this trek that there was an end to this journey, and at that end, there would come the conquered and the victorious." Coach Beasley pauses a moment and glances around the room into every one of his player's eyes, making that personal connection mentally and speaking to each heart and continues his speech. "By not being successful in completing that task and getting it done, we are the warriors on that side of defeat. We are human, so it hurts, and yeah, it sucks! Now I say 'warriors' because after giving away a twenty-five-point lead in the first half of a road playoff game, the crowd were vigorously enthused and active as they were tonight. You had every reason to hang your heads, start blaming and fighting one another for mistakes, and just throw in the towel. From the start of the second half, every bit of it was about character. You strapped your boots up and dug into the grind of the game as if the score were back at zero to zero, and the first half did not matter. We started playing like ourselves. We got disciplined on defense, and our intensity picked up, which helped us on our own little run. Those Eagles' fans got nervous when we brought the score to within one point. True warriors you were tonight, gentlemen—champions in heart showing great character by leaving everything out there on the floor this evening. We made too many costly decisions at the start of the game and ran out of time in the end. Time is the most precious. We can never get it back. Once it is gone, it is gone. We can only be wise and be more efficient and effective with it as we grow with the seasons. Be humble, my young warriors, as you continue the journey through the changing seasons of life and be wise on how you choose to be effective with your time. Defeat does not taste well on the lips, so remember it. Use it. Strive and push yourselves to limits when perfecting your craft, not just in the game of basketball but in all aspects of life. In the off-season, we know this is when we get better, not during the season, so we will be discussing the off-season training schedule and getting that out to you guys in about a week. We figured that should be enough downtime for you guys to have a little break, rest up, and take care of the aches and bangs to your bodies. To you seniors, it has been one hell of a ride with you guys this season. I love the heck out of you guys, and I will do anything in the world for you to get to that next level of life. Always players of mine, we have a lot more business to discuss as far as the future and upcoming school options. For now though, I am going to go ahead and wrap this up and let you guys get showered and freshened up so that we can begin this three-hour ride back home."

The coach calls to the group. "Bring it in, fellas! Big Dee, come on. We are going to have you lead and break us down one last time for the season."

Big Dee towers the middle of the encircled players and coaches. With his arm raised high, hand in fist, Big Dee bellows, "Let's go, Raiders. On three, let's go, Raiders. On three…1, 2, 3!"

All the players and coaches shout in unison "Let's go, Raiders!"

*****

Ronin and Paul while exiting out of the locker room after showering are chatting about the game.

"Man, I hate taking losses. We had that too! Now we must go back to the city, lame and stuff. We almost won, so that shouldn't mess up my status with the ladies, right?" moans Paul.

Ronin throws an amusing glance at his best friend. "Almost does not count, and maybe, that is the reason your game was a little off, focusing on the ladies, *playa*!"

Paul shoves Ronin in a friendly manner and says, "Ah, don't be a hater, Ronin. I'm just saying I must keep all my skills together, my all-around game. You feel me? Can you tell me this? Is it me, or does Coach Beasley always sound like some old kung fu master from the Shaolin temple in his end-of-the game speeches?"

As if Paul had just read the mind of his friend Ronin, the two friends glare at each other before they begin in chuckles of laughter. "I most agree with you on that one, like he caught the Bruce Lee marathon on this weekend," Ronin adds. "This felt like our year. Hate that we let this one get away. We are next in line to lead the team, and next year is not promised that we will even make it this far. There is no choice but to step it up and go hard the entire off-season and summer. I'm talking basketball twenty-four seven."

"Most definitely all-day every day, homey!" inserts Paul.

As Ronin and Paul approach the end of the hallway, they observe the number of Raiders fans waiting to give their comments and after-game love before the ride home. A strong but sweet voice from the distance can be heard.

"Ronin, Ronin!" shouts the voice in an excited tone from above the crowd. Ronin seeks and discovers his target among lingering fans—his mother, Keisha—as she presses forward through the mob of people in their direction. She reaches to embrace her son. Ronin returns his mother's embrace as she speaks.

"Great game. It was not the prettiest, but it still was a great game! You all did not give up," she comments.

Ronin exhibits a demoralized stare at the ground. "Does not feel so great on the losing end, Mom. should have done better."

Keisha reaches for Ronin's chin and raises it so that his eyes met her eyes and says, "Boy, pick your head up. What do you have your head down for? You have nothing to be ashamed about. You went out there and did the best you could do, son!" As a single African American mother raising a young African American man in urban South Florida, Keisha tries to be encouraging and guiding in the upbringing of both her children. Ronin is the eldest of the two, his sister's senior by two years.

"Hi, Ms. Miller!" salutes Paul.

"Hey, Paul, good job out there trying to bring it home! But hey, you win some and you lose some, but you live to fight on another day!" replies Ms. Miller.

"Excuses me, Ms. Miller. But did you just quote the dad from the movie *Friday*?" asks Paul.

"Yes, I did," answers Ms. Miller.

They all join in the laughter. Ronin starts the conversation again. "Ma, where is Iesha?" he asks, scanning the crowd for his younger sister and looking forward to hearing her post-game remarks on his performance.

"She went to the restroom," replies his mom, and then a *smack* from behind the head of Ronin.

"The game has got you slipping, bro!" In comes Iesha, always witty and on her toes to jump at an opportunity to joke or prank her elder sibling, reminding him on how much she adores her older brother.

"Oh, enters Queen B-i-t-c-h! She graces us with her presence!" declares Ronin in a humorous manner.

"Ronin!" shouts Ms. Miller, and like snatching a fly out of thin air—*smack*—it is another slap to the back of the head of the high school junior, but this time, it is from his quick-handed mother. "Don't call your sister a bitch!"

"Did the best you all could do, huh?" begins Iesha.

Ronin's response is "Yeah, I guess you can say that. It was just not enough, little sister."

"Don't be so hard on yourself, Ronin. Twelve points, nine rebounds, two blocks, and three steals was not a bad performance. I think that was a pretty solid game. You guys got much farther than my school, so I cannot say much. Plus, you did not do anything goofy tonight. I was kind of upset a bit that you did not give me any new material. What's up, Paul? Good game. Too bad you chumps could not bring the win home."

"Hey, Iesha, what's up? So what is my stat line, Stephen A. Smith?" Paul asks, joking around with Iesha.

Ronin now chimes in, "Yeah, ESPN, were those my numbers tonight? You keep numbers better than the *Providencia Post*."

Iesha responds quickly, "Oh, shut up. You know you wanted to know any way. You should thank me, and shouldn't you two be preparing to load up to head back?"

"I think we were some of the first guys out of the locker room, so actually, I think we are just waiting on the rest of the guys to come out," explains Ronin.

"Speaking on heading back," blurts Paul, "Ms. Miller, my mom had to work graveyard shift tonight. That's why she couldn't make it to the game. I want to know if it is OK to bum a ride from you to my house?"

Paul is the second-oldest child of five in a single-parent household. His mother works two different jobs, picking up extra shifts when she can. Ms. Griggs and Ms. Miller are good friends from childhood, so it is no problem for the two women to be supportive and help each other out in a time of need. Ms. Miller turns to Paul and places her hand on his shoulders while saying, "Of course, Paul. You know you can always ride with us. You are like one of my own too!"

Ronin and Paul are now expressing grins of joy. Then the group proceeds to engage in their departing routines before they split and go their ways. Ronin and Paul head toward the team bus, passing through the lingering crowd of spectators. Ms. Miller and Iesha are off in the direction to their vehicle to head back south. Back at the bus and now checking in their bags with the bus driver, Ronin and Paul listen as he gives his remarks on tonight's contest.

"Sorry about the loss, fellas! But you guys did make it a good one in the end," says the driver as he loads the players' luggage underneath the bus. "Plus, the two of you are just juniors. I can only imagine how you will do next season. Who knows I may be talking to some future NBA prospects!"

"I would most definitely take that big check and shoe deal from Nike," replies Paul.

"Ronin." A voice calls from behind the bus, startling the group and interrupting the conversation between the players and the bus driver. Ronin, recognizing the figure of his father, steps out from behind the bus and comes his way.

"Pops, what's up? What are you doing here?" asks Ronin.

"One of the biggest games in the boy's career so far and you think that I would not be here to see that? Come on now," states Ronin's father. "What's happening with you, champ? How are you living?" Father and son reach their arms for a handshake and embrace.

"I'm doing OK. Would have been much better if we got the win," utters Ronin.

"I can understand that. I came into the game just before halftime, and you guys were down and climbing in an uphill battle. The team came out much more settled in the second half. You did some good things, made some plays, and had a positive impact on the game. I enjoyed watching you compete at your highest level and play through adversity. It had me admiring how much your skills have improved over the years. It kills me missing that time away from Iesha and you. I know you are hurting right now about the loss, but as you know, this is the road of the warrior. Either you win or you lose. You can sit and cry about it, or you can go to work and get better. I've always said to you before, your life is much bigger than any game. There are far greater things out there for you to contribute. This is far from the end of the road for you, so don't get so down about it!"

Ronin and his father are having a rare moment because of the fact that they have seen less of each other over the years. Ronin and Iesha's parents have not always agreed on a lot of things, so they can get into some heated arguments. They have never been married, so it is just best for the two to co-parent, with Keisha having full custody.

"I was talking with Iesha during the game. I see she is still keeping you on your toes, just how little sisters are supposed to," says Ronin's father.

"Never missing an opportunity," adds Ronin.

They hear chatter from Ronin's remaining teammates, emerging out of the group of family members saying their goodbyes.

"Well, let me not keep you from your teammates. You all have a long ride back home tonight. We will get together later and talk some more X's and O's." Ronin's father looks at his boy. "Love you, kid. Keep pushing yourself, and remember, your bloodline is greater than you know!"

"Love you too, Dad," Ronin returns his father's expression as the two shake hands, hug, and depart from each other.

Ronin turns to catch up with Paul, who's already settled on the bus and prepared for the ride home with an empty seat beside him. "Saved the window seat for you, bro," says Paul.

"Appreciate it," answers Ronin, removing his MP3 player from his backpack, then proceeds to pack the inside of the overhead compartment, and then takes his seat by the window; his remaining teammates are now loading their luggage and filing into their places on the bus. As the players take their seats, assistant coach Franks quiets the chattering bunch.

"Quiet it up for a minute, guys, just a quick roll call, and then we will be on our way. The plan is to stop for food and what not before we get on the highway, which is about fifteen minutes away. We know you guys are hungry. So let's get this process done and over with."

Ronin shuffles through his favorite OutKast playlist during Coach Franks's roll call.

"Brown, Cummings."

Players are raising a hand, acknowledging the coach.

"Drummond."

"Here," responds Ronin and raises his hand.

"Oh, and by the way, it is supposed to get a little nasty with the weather on the ride back. We are riding through a thunderstorm," announces the coach.

"Thunderstorm or not, I am ready for food. Beef would be nice," moans Paul, rubbing his stomach at the same time.

Ronin is staring out of the window. "I'm just ready to relax, take my mind off the game, and try not to beat myself up about it," says Ronin. Ronin adjusts each of his earbuds into his ears, finds the song titled "Myintrotoletyouknow," hits Play, tilts his head back, and fades into a heavy sleep. At the same time, the storm clouds begin to roll as the team makes their trip south in the night.

CHAPTER 2

A MYSTICAL AND POWERFUL VOICE comes like a whisper, "Will you be the one? Will you be the one? You must choose. You must choose! The roots of the ancestral tree are being cut. The roots of the ancestral tree are being cut! Mother Ethiopia cries. Mother Ethiopia cries. Will you be the one? You must choose!"

A rolling sea of enormous storm clouds, together with shattering cracks of lightning, bolts across the skies, shifting its formation. The cloud begins to materialize in the form of a wolf. A mystic voice utters, "How can a man know himself without knowing his history? The knowledge of the past must never be forgotten!"

Beep! Beep! Beep! Beep!

Ronin jerks awake, startled by the blaring alarm clock. His undershirt is drenched in a cold sweat. He's wearing a puzzled look on his face.

"Man, I must have been out. I don't remember anything after getting on the bus," he said aloud, noticing that he has overslept into his alarm's call for fifteen minutes. Ronin hurries into the shower to prepare for the day. To cut time, Ronin grabs his toothbrush and toothpaste, vigorously stroking his pearly and white teeth, next cleaning his body. Out of the shower, feeling fresh and energized, Ronin collects his school uniform—a navy-blue polo-style shirt with the school's initials embroidered over the left chest plate, khaki pants, and a pair of loafers; he then snatches his backpack and proceeds out of the room.

In the kitchen of the three-bedroom apartment, Keisha, who's at the stove already arranging breakfast on plates, announces that the meals are ready. "Ronin! Iesha! Ya'll better hurry up and get a move on it. The food is ready. I am not taking anybody to school this morning, so ya'll better make it to ya'll bus!"

Iesha enters the kitchen as her mother sets the breakfast plates on the table. "Morning, Ma," says Iesha as she takes her seat at the table. "I see slowpoke still has not gotten up."

"Good morning, Iesha. No, Ronin has not gotten his butt in here yet. He is still tired from last night. But he better get his butt in here. After all that driving last night, I still beat ya'll two up and made breakfast."

"Ya'll talking about me?" Ronin's voice echoes in. He is now walking into the room filled with the smell of freshly cooked bacon, eggs, and pancakes.

"Good morning, boy. You were out like a log last night. We damn near had to carry you into the house," responds Ronin's mom.

Ronin replies, "Yeah, I had to be. I don't even remember getting here or to the school last night."

Keisha teases, "My back sure does remember. You are not a little boy anymore," as she rubs her lower back.

"Talk about the walking dead," chimes in Iesha, as she helps herself to a hearty portion of eggs.

"I still can't believe we lost that game last night," sighs Ronin as he makes his path toward his mother and then gives her a kiss on the cheek.

"Good morning, Ma!" He then grabs a slice of bacon from his breakfast plate on the table and takes a bite. He then greets his sister with a kiss on her forehead, saying, "Good morning, little sis," then takes his seat across the kitchen table from Iesha.

"Being upset about losing the game is OK. You should be, but don't spend too much time beating yourself up about it. You can't waste time pouting," says Keisha.

"Well, seems to me like someone has some motivational fuel to burn this off-season. Go hard or go home," Iesha shares, adding to the conversation as she chomps down on her pancakes. "You will be all right. You know you can sit and cry about it or go get better. Easier said than done, but I know you are not the crying type, and besides, it was just last night."

Keisha, now taking a sip of her freshly brewed coffee, says, "Your sister is right. All this is going to do is push you. We all need that push sometimes. Like now, I need to push myself to go get ready, and you two need to not miss ya'll bus." Kiesha wipes down the kitchen counter while the two siblings consume what's on their morning plates. "Now that I have gotten ya'll out of the way, I can go now and get myself together." Keisha then leans in and places a kiss on the cheek of Iesha. Swiftly going around the table, she moves, placing a kiss on the forehead of Ronin. Before scurrying out of the kitchen to prepare for her day, she emphasizes, "I have a meeting tonight after work, so I will be late getting in. It will most likely be around 8:30–9:00 p.m. Please make sure that you two have your house keys, Ronin. I love ya'll. Make the most of ya'll day!" Then out of the kitchen she goes.

Iesha completes her plate before her brother. "Come on, slow-poke. Hurry up."

Ronin, chewing on his bacon, contests, "Slowpoke? It takes time to have this much swag. I thought you knew that." Ronin finishes up his last bite.

"Well, I'm not sure about your swag and all that, but I do know that we have a bus to get to, and it comes in about thirty minutes. We still have a fifteen-minute walk to get there, so I don't know about you, but I am heading out the door."

Ronin, not noticing the time, gives chase after his younger sister as she goes out of the front door, soon following behind. Ronin steps outside just as the morning sun rises above the horizon of downtown Providencia Beach's Skyline.

"Shoot! I forgot my jacket," moans Iesha.

"Look who's talking about being a slowpoke, at least, I remembered my keys," teases Ronin. "Why do you need your jacket. It's not that cold, and besides, by the time it's twelve o'clock, you are going to burn."

"Yeah, you only remembered your keys because Ma reminded you, and not everybody burns like an inferno like you. I will be right back." Iesha sprints back inside their house to retrieve her jacket. Ronin takes a moment to appreciate his view.

The sight of the sun is beautiful—its burnt umber-red rays blended with swirls of varied hues of blue, white, pink, and yellow; dew produce in the night's condensation is gleaming from blades of grass. Outside temperature is around sixty-five degrees before the sun rises and begins to heat up. The sounds of the traffic in the distance are heard as the city begins to wake up and become active. Breaking his moment of peace, a screeching sound just about gives him a heart attack. "Whoop! Whoop! Whoop! Whoop! Whoop!" Ronin notices a massive-sized bird with a menacing appearance perched up on a streetlight. It's unlike any other bird he has seen before in the city limits. He knows the creature is not native to the area.

"Whoop," calls the large bird while eyeing the teenage boy in just as much curiosity.

"OK, got it. Let's rock."

Out comes Iesha snuggly fitted into her favorite Miami Heat hoodie.

"Hey, Iesha, check this out!" Ronin nudges his head in the direction of the winged animal.

"Wow! That's huge. What kind of a bird is that?" Iesha says with her eyes amazed by the sight.

"I know that. It can't be from around here. It's a bird of prey," states Ronin.

"A bird of what?" asks Iesha, expressing a perplexed look on her face.

"A bird of prey, a raptor," answers Ronin.

"But aren't raptors the dinosaurs who hunt in packs in the movie *Jurassic Park*?" questions Iesha.

"Yeah, those are called raptors also, which are birds that evolved from dinosaurs millions of years ago by losing their teeth and growing beaks. But these raptors are a species of bird that hunt and feed on mostly animals that are relatively larger than its size—birds like eagles, falcons, and hawks," explains Ronin.

"I definitely need to tune in more to the Discovery Channel with you. By the size of that thing, it looks like it can hunt anything it wants. I just hope it's not us," mutters Iesha.

"It's not hunting us," reassures Ronin, "but I don't know why a raptor of that size is here in South Florida. It could be someone's pet that got out." Ronin reaches in his right pants pocket then pulls out his Moto G7 smartphone and takes a snapshot of the bird. The flash from the camera startles the bird and sends it into the air, calling, "Whoop! Whoop!"

With a flap of his wings, the bird rises. The beat of the winds whistling through its wings carries clearly in dawn's silence. They are standing in astonishment at the grace of the large bird and at how swift and strong the bird ascended into the air. The raptor spreads its massive wings wider than the length of its body, then advances into the morning wind and flies off into the horizon of the sun.

"That was wicked awesome!" screams Iesha. "You got that on your camera?"

Ronin feels as much excitement in the sighting as his younger sister does, stamping a memorable moment between the two that shall surpass a lifetime. "Yeah, that's awesome, but we better get a move on it before we both miss the bus." Ronin and Iesha begin their trek to the bus stop.

The two take two different routes: Ronin taking the city bus across town to Cardinal Huemen private school on an athletic scholarship and Iesha traveling uptown to Boris Hill High School, not on scholarship but ahead one year in grade and taking all advanced classes. Ronin takes pride in walking with his little sister to the bus stop, having only so much time during the day to spend with each other. They try to make the most out of walking together. Ronin loves his little sister, and he is ready to protect her at all cost. Iesha loves her older brother as well; she appreciates the guidance, his protective nature, and even though she knows he does not have it altogether at moments, she is still his biggest fan and she is ready to fight for him at all cost. But little did the siblings know that they are coming to their destiny's crossroads and that they will soon have to make some fundamental decisions that will put that love to the test.

They make it to their destination with about eight minutes to spare, give or take. The buses are running on schedule.

"Youngblood," calls out an older man in uniform waiting at the bus stop, "getting li'l sis to the bus stop on time as usual."

"What's up, Chauncey," greets Ronin and Iesha. Chauncey is about twenty-one years old, and he lives in the neighborhood. He is that person in the hood that knows just about any and every current event going on in the city, being what he likes to call a "hood entrepreneur." Chauncey deals with a network of all sort of different business ventures. Often, he and Ronin talks and debates about the latest sport news. Chauncey has made a name for himself playing basketball in high school and in college a few semesters. He always stresses to Ronin on how he made decisions to explore other less prestigious skills of his. Ronin feels that Chauncey always attempting to warn him against the temptations of the streets is his way of trying to atone for some of the past mistakes in his life.

"Heard about the game last night. Sorry about the loss, but don't worry about it. You still got game. Twelve points, nine rebounds, two blocks, and three steals—you were hooping. Ya'll just can't turn the ball over like that and expect to win."

"Yeah, thanks. Were you at the game last night?" asks Ronin, raising an eyebrow.

"Nah, I wasn't at the game last night. You know me, blood. I have my connections, but it's all good. You're still my li'l dude," replies Chauncey.

"By the way, what's up with the uniform? You get another job?" asks Iesha.

"You know me, li'l sis. I have my hustles, and I can't leave these streets alone, but I did pick up a part-time gig on the morning-shift loading," answers Chauncey.

"There goes my bus," announces Iesha as the large rectangular vehicle's brakes loudly grinded to a stop. "Congratulations on your new gig, Chauncey," says Iesha.

"Thank you, li'l sis. See you later. Keep knocking out those books," he returns.

"Thank you. Have a good one, OK?"

She turns to her brother and reaches to give him a hug. Ronin leans down to hug his sister. She whispers in Ronin's ear, "Have a great day and don't let anyone get to you. I love you, bro."

"I love you too, sis. Be the best you can be!"

Iesha hops on to the bus and finds herself a window seat. She then waves as the bus departed. Chauncey reengages in conversation. "Li'l sis is a freshman in sophomore classes, and she is wearing big boy pants!"

"Yeah, she's tough. She is a hell of a lot more disciplined in her studies than me. She can handle the pressure well."

"I feel you, but high school is a different type of beast, especially without big bro there," responds Chauncey.

"Even when I'm not with her, I am always with her," says Ronin in a firm tone. Chauncey senses the change in Ronin's energy.

"Calm down, Tyson. I know you got li'l sis. I was just saying cats in high school can be treacherous."

Ronin is thankful to have the view of his bus coming up from the horizon of approaching traffic to cut the tension of the conversation, knowing that even though Chauncey is standing at the bus stop, he never gets on and rides the bus. He is just there for the business location.

"Well, all right, youngblood, I see your chariot has arrived."

Ronin reaches his hand to part ways with his older comrade, to make his way across town. "All right, Chauncey, take it easy!"

"Do your thing, blood. I'll catch up to you later!"

The Providencia city bus arrives just five minutes after the departure of his younger sister. Ronin reaches into his pocket, pulling out his wallet to fumble through and collect his fare.

"Ronin, good morning. Superstar, how did it go last night?" happily greets the bus driver, Mr. Wright.

"Good morning, Mr. Wright. The superstar is not feeling all too super right now. We didn't play our best first half of basketball, and we got ourselves in trouble early," Ronin replies, describing the details of the game as he slid two of his crisp dollar bills and two quarters into the coin machine.

Mr. Wright, persistent in his encouraging words to his young rider, says, "Keep your head up, young buck. You have a lot more game left in you. Just keep doing your thing and stay positive. You are one of the top athletes in the area. Don't get down on yourself!"

"Thanks for the pep talk, Mr. Wright."

"Anytime, young brother, like I said, head up!"

Ronin continues to make his way to find his usual seat on the almost vacant bus as any other morning. The only other person on the bus besides Mr. Wright and Ronin was an older homeless gentleman sleeping in the opposite window seat in the back of the bus, niched tightly in his corner. Shuffling through his media player's track list, Ronin finds one of his favorite songs to uplift him when he gets into a slump, "The Optimistic" by a gospel choir Sounds of Blackness. He then plugs in his headphones and tries to relax as the bus cruised on to the next stop.

Two or three stops into the ride across town, a group of rowdy teenagers got on the bus making jokes and clowning around, and they just so happen to choose to sit in the seats just ahead of the gentlemen sleeping. Ronin pays little attention to the boys' commotion. Seeming like the bunch has the intentions to cause mischief, they turn their focus of jokes toward the homeless man. Ronin attempts his best not to be bothered by the situation, understanding how boys can be, especially boys at their ages—they could be no more than fourteen or fifteen.

The homeless man is completely minding his own business, just trying to take advantage of the shelter from the bus to get some rest. One could most definitely see that this man has been through some hard times. His ragged, unshaven face sprouts gray and white hairs. His head is full of shapely black-and-white dreadlocks. His clothes are weathered and stained from living outside, in the elements, causing him to have a rancid smell of musk and sweat. A nice hot shower and a good shave are long overdue, but nonetheless, should a person's humanity and dignity be taken for granted by others because of their current circumstances, most certainly in cases when dealing with elders? The man is now fully awoken by the ridiculing bunch of boys.

Ronin, now at full attention to the situation, ponders to him-self, *With all the sacrifices made by the elders back in the day—slavery, lynching, and the civil rights movement—just to be able to ride the bus freely, and here we have here in modern America a group of young black boys cracking jokes and making fun of one of their own elders. I can only imagine how Dr. King or Mrs. Parks will react to what I am seeing right now.* Ronin, longer able to contain himself, swiftly moves into action. "So picking on people's grandparents is what ya'll call having fun or being cool?" Ronin addresses the group in a challenging manner.

It's an unexpected interruption of their comedy show. They have not taken notice of the other passenger. Oddly enough, one of the smallest of the group—a scrawny kid medium in height, some-where around five feet four inches, and wearing jeans that's a pants size too large and in need of a belt, an extra-large and too wide black T-shirt, and a gold necklace around his neck—postures himself to respond to Ronin's objection.

Ronin takes the gesture as him being the alpha of the group.

"He isn't my daddy, and who the hell are you any, super save a nigga!" protests the leader.

"And if I was, what are ya'll going to do about it?" spits back Ronin as he grows more aggressive in his tone. "The fact of the mat-ter is that he is someone's uncle, father, son, or grandfather! How would you feel if someone were doing it to one of your parents or grandparents? You would be ready to fight, right? This man didn't do a thing to ya'll. Why be cowards and go mess with him? Can't ya'll do something more constructive with ya'll time?"

Like little puppies tucking their hind sides, the alpha and his group of lackeys grow small with shame and intimidation from the imposing tone and speech from Ronin. Without hesitation, the alpha turns and heads to the front of the bus with his entourage following suit.

"Thank you, young man," says the older gentleman, expressing his gratitude. "Most people these days wouldn't have even spoken to me, let alone step in to defend me."

"No thanks needed," Ronin says, modestly speaking. "It just frustrated me that those guys went out of their way to come bother an elder person, someone who was not even paying attention to them. They have no respect!"

"I do not blame them," states the man. "I pity them, for they do not understand the rage that runs within them. My young king, our people have been so beat down, divided up, and concerned with current problems that we have forgotten the importance of the bond between our youth and elders." The gentleman is now in a deep daze, as if reminiscing on times past.

The bus is now coming to Ronin's stop, just a quarter mile from the high school. "Well, here is my stop. It was nice talking to you, unfortunate the situation might be," says Ronin. Before making his exit from the bus, Ronin whips out his billfold and takes out five dollars of the fifteen that he has remaining and hands it to the older gentleman. "I wish I could do more," expresses Ronin.

The man takes Ronin's hand. "Young king, you have done more than you know." Ronin then turns to exit the bus, walking past his crowd of hecklers as they now sit talking among themselves, unfazed by the altercation.

"See you later, Superstar," salutes Mr. Wright. "Until tomorrow!"

Ronin begins his trek to the small high school campus that's surrounded by a nice suburban neighborhood, small shopping plazas, various restaurants, and gas stations. With the bus stop being close to the school and Ronin being one of the top role players on the basketball team, he never makes it to the school walking. There is always a fellow student riding by and spotting him and insists on offering him a lift. Right on time, as Ronin heads toward the school, he can hear the booming of loud music and screeching tires coming up from behind him in the distance and growing louder in its approach.

"You mighta've seen me in the streets, but, nigga, you don't know me. When you holla, when you speak, remember you don't know me. Save all the hatin' and the poppin', nigga. You don't know me. Quit tellin' niggaz you my partna, nigga. You don't know me!"

Ronin already knows who the driver of the vehicle is from the voice of the rap artist TI coming from the loudspeakers. "What's up, fool? You still walking?" Ronin turns to see two of his teammates:

Erik driving his Jeep Wrangler and always listening to TI and Paul hanging outside of the passenger window.

"Not you two chumps this early!" teases Ronin.

"So are you riding or what?" asks Paul.

Ronin jumps in the back seat of the jeep. "It's six o'clock in the morning just after a loss and leave it to you two to start the block party," shouts Ronin as the comrades ride to school.

As the three companions walk through the campus from the student parking lot, they parade past various groups of chattering students, greeting them as they come through. The group comes to find majority of the team hanging out in their regular hallway section right in the middle of the two-story corridor.

"Ronin, EA Sports, PG, what's up homeys?" Big Dee greets them, holding down his post.

"Big Dee, what it do?" Paul returns, setting off a chain of high fives and handshakes.

"Man, that *L* last night was the worse. Fuck all that we came back and all, but that shyt hurts!" moans Big Dee.

"I still can't feel my legs," grumbles Erik.

"Yeah, yeah, but forget about that for right now. We have more important matters to be discussing right now, states Paul.

"What could be more important than last night's game right now?" asks Ronin.

Paul gladly answers, "Are ya'll going to Byron's block party tonight?"

"Byron from John I?" inquires Erik.

"Yeah, Byron, from John I," answers Paul.

"Oh, everybody is going to be there. It's going to be thick—biggest party this year. Ya'll got to go," exclaims Big Dee, stressing the importance of the social event, as far as the lives of teenagers go.

"That's the problem. Some of everybody is going to be there," murmurs Ronin, not showing the same excitement about the mixer as the other guys.

"Ah, come on, Ron. Man, don't do that. The season is over. We have some downtime. This is not the time to start being all depressed," pleads Paul. "This is the best part of the school year. Don't worry about the game last night. We can get together this weekend and get some shots up. Come on, bro. Peer pressure, peer pressure!" Paul jokes around.

"All right, man, all right," Ronin says, not so enthused as he gives in to the crowds' request.

"Squad!" yells Paul.

The bunch shakes hands in celebration of Ronin agreeing.

Ring, ring, ring! Sounds the first bell to begin homeroom classes. The procrastinating teenagers chat on a few minutes, not being too hasty to get to homeroom on time.

"At least, I will be the responsible one and get to class on time," Ronin cuts in to break from the small chatter, "see you guys later!"

"Be easy, my boy," salutes Big Dee, not breaking much concentration while in conversation with a wide-eyed classmate talking about the game.

Ronin heads down the hallway, just wishing to get to class and talk as less as possible about the game. He cuts around the corner and starts walking up the twisted staircase to the second level of the building, and not even midway up, he hears the stampeding feet of Paul trying to catch up with him.

"Thought you were going to just ride out another detention session with Mr. Bachman," says Ronin, as he makes his strides up the last steps.

Paul, soon catching up to his lead, replies, "Nah, I actually figured I would finally follow your lead on this one," responds Paul as they made it to the doors of Mrs. Henderson's homeroom class.

The boys enter the classroom filled with students sitting prepared for morning announcements and having conversations. They, too, file into their assigned seats to await roll call and the start of the morning news.

Meanwhile, across town, stuck on her school bus as it moves through morning traffic, Iesha is singing one of her favorite Monica songs "Don't Take It Personal," "It's just one of dem days that a girl goes through / When I'm angry inside, don't want to take it out on you / Just one of dem days, don't take it personal / I just wanna be all alone." The bus inches into the school's bus-loop entrance. Iesha gathers up her belongings as the bus comes to its stop. She waits for a good time to hop into position in the line of quickly exiting students. As she exits the bus, Iesha neatly wraps her headphones around her cell phone, shuts down her device, and stores it away in her backpack as she dodges through the traffic of flowing students entering the school.

"Good morning, students! Great to see you here, ready to go!" Iesha hears up ahead Mr. Lockhart, her English teacher on post, giving his morning greetings and motivational quotes of the day. "Hey, hey, Jermaine, my man." Mr. Lockhart gives out high fives to students as they pass. "Good morning, Iesha," Mr. Lockhart greets Iesha as she approaches.

"Good morning, Mr. Lockhart. How are you doing today?" Iesha greets her English teacher.

"I am doing quite well, and I was just thinking of you." Iesha, unsure of the coming comments, feels her insides drop for a moment as a nervous sensation was sent throughout her body. "I was very impressed on how you presented and argued your perspective in your paper 'The Origin of Democracy via the African Constitution.' You exceeded my expectations. I really enjoyed how you discussed in detail the body of fundamental theories, principles, and practices within African societies in its earliest times. You are most definitely the scholar student!"

Iesha takes a giant breath of relief. "Oh, man, I just got so nervous, right then. Iesha exhales, holding her chest.

Mr. Lockhart asks, "Why nervous?"

Iesha replies, "I thought something was wrong. I worked so hard on that paper. I even cut into some allowance to buy the books to write it."

"Well, it most definitely showed. Well done. I say continue on your path. You have great potential," compliments the teacher.

Jolts of joy are now firing off through Iesha's body from Mr. Lockhart's words of encouragement. Iesha is now reenergized in her strides through the corridors of the school's hallway en route to the student lockers to gather her belongings for the day. She contemplates over her day's agenda. "Today is day A, so I am going to need my math, biology, and history books and my gym shorts and shirt for gym class." Iesha bends to a corner and comes into the hall where her locker is located.

"Oh great, now I have to deal with these guys!" Iesha finds her locker being occupied as this morning's hangout area to some of the more infamous upperclassmen of the school—a few faces she recognized from around the neighborhood that had some buzz about street gang activity and a few of the boys she knew played basketball either with or against her brother Ronin and his friend Paul in grade school. Iesha has never paid any attention to their names because most of them are rarely in school on a consistent basis. They were usually here on game days or hanging around early morning and during lunchtime. The group of boys' attentions are all concentrated on their gossip and jovial laughter as Iesha makes her presence known to excuse herself.

"Excuse me, guys...hi. Can I just get by you to grab my books?" Iesha says, being most polite in her interruption.

"Excuse me, li'l mama. We didn't mean to hold you up," answers one of the upperclassmen as the bunch steered their attentions toward Iesha. This upperclassman clearly had the most charisma and superior character among his crews.

"It's really fine. I just don't want to be late to class," replies Iesha.

"I don't want you to be late to class either. Can I walk you to class? I promise I'll get you there on time." The upperclassman signals to his comrades to clear a path. "You must be new. This is my first time seeing you. Are you a freshman?"

Iesha, a little impatient in her reply, says, "Yes, I am new to the school this year, and I would be a freshman, but I was advanced a grade, so I am a sophomore."

"Damn, fresh meat, smart, and sexy too. You sure I can't walk you to class?" again asks the upperclassman.

Iesha quickly responds, now expressing that her patience is being tested, "I'm positive. I would like to just get my books so that I can get to class on time."

He senses the intense energy coming from Iesha. "I'm sorry. I'm not trying to get you upset and make you uncomfortable. I will see you later, fresh meat." The upperclassman leads himself and his peanut gallery away as they made their comments.

"Like dogs in heat, but I'm more than a piece of meat." Iesha proceeds to gather her things and refocus on the day's tasks.

*****

"She thinks she is all that!" comments Tammy, a classmate of Iesha, who was well trained in the art of playing possum. As she witnesses the interaction of her fellow schoolmates.

"Who are you talking about, Tammy?" response the friend of the jealous watcher.

"Iesha. She thinks she is so smart, and just because her brother plays ball at some private school, she thinks she is better than us."

"How do you know she thinks she is better than us? I just thought she was just a nerd, but her brother looks good though, and he has some game."

"Kenia, he is OK, but he is not that special," argues Tammy.

"Was Tony just over there talking to her too?"

"Tony does not want that girl, Sheena," barks Tammy at her friend.

"I'm just saying. Of all people, you know how Tony is," states Sheena.

"Yeah, I know how Tony is," replies Tammy.

Unaware of the watching pack of girls having their morning gossip, wherein she just so happens to be the topic of discussion, Iesha casually organizes her math, biology, and history books within her backpack and then folds her gym uniform, then places it on top of her books. Securing her locker and zipper on her pack, Iesha returns to the traffic of streaming students.

"Ring!" The school bell sounds, alarming the students of their fifteen minutes to the start of first period.

OK, let's just hope the rest of today goes by drama-free, Iesha thinks to herself. By passing the hall, Iesha notices three of her classmates, which she has been making acquaintance.

"Hey, Iesha girl, good morning!"

"Good morning, Tammy, Kenia, Sheena. How ya'll doing?" greets Iesha.

"Hey, Iesha," greets Kenia and Sheena.

"We were just talking about you," admits Tammy.

"Oh yeah? What were you saying about me?" asks Iesha.

"We were just saying that none of us understands how to do these math equations like you do, so we wanted to know if you could try starting a study group with us." Tammy pleads her and her classmates' case.

Iesha feels like she was being put on the spot. "I am really not the study group-type, but I guess giving it a try can't be so bad. It at least beats falling asleep by myself over world history," Iesha agrees.

"That's what we are talking about," cheers the group of girls.

"But we better get to class first before we are late," says Iesha, joining the bunch as they walk to class.

"So, Iesha, are you coming to the party tonight?" asks Kenia.

Iesha is not too big into the social life at school beyond books and study; any of her other free time is spent usually running after her brother Ronin and his best friend Paul on one of their unexpected adventures. "No, what party?" asks Iesha.

"Girl, Byron's block party. It's going to be so crazy!" says Kenia.

"Byron who?" asks Iesha.

"One of the upperclassmen at John I. Byron is having a block party tonight, and everybody is going to be there," explains Sheena.

"I can tell from the enthusiasm that this is a big deal. I'm usually hanging out with my brother on Friday nights. I will have to see what he has planned," Iesha replies.

"Oh, your brother, doesn't he play ball at another school?" asks Tammy.

"Yeah, he plays at a private school, but their season ended last night, so I'm not sure if he will be up for a party or not," states Iesha.

"Well, I sure hope you do come out because you never hang out with us," cries Tammy.

The group of girls reaches the door of their first period Math class at the sound of the five-minute bell ring.

"Come and sit in the back with us. You always sit in the front. We won't bite you back here," insists Kenia.

Iesha does not want to be rude and turn down the invitation, and besides, she feels a little joy inside to have someone else besides her brother and his friend Paul wanting to hang out with her. "I guess a switch to the back today won't hurt." Iesha then heads to the back of the classroom, finding her seat in the middle of her associates as they chat and prepare for the start of class.

CHAPTER 3

TEN THOUSAND YEARS AFTER THE second Ice Age of Pangea, in some remote region in the land of Ethiopia, Father Universe, the supreme energy in all creation of life; and his consort Mother Nature, the mother of all living things, engage in conversation. A thunderous and celestial voice speaks.

"Mother Nature, it has been quite the millennia. Our children of the earth have gradually adapted to their surrounding environments, diet, and lifestyle. Through your bond and guidance, man's intelligence have enabled him to succeed and survive in the harsh, cold climates. Mastering and understanding fire's life essence has allowed them to become healthier by cooking food, as well as keep them safe and protected by providing light and heat, along with the furs of animals, in the night. In their lessons of craftsmanship, they have become artisans of stone tools, migrating during the various seasons searching for food. The children of the earth's nomadic life has been an everyday struggle to find enough food to feed the group. The bond between the natural forces, along with practicing exercises of meditation, has developed their conscious control of spirit essence, therefore enabling them to develop powers that lay hidden in all man. It is time for a new challenge and task due our sons and daughters," expresses Father Universe.

"Yes, Father Universe, our children have indeed grown in their intelligence. It was not so long ago that they came from my sands, and you breathed life into them. It is time for them to further their understanding of life's mysteries. Our sons and daughters will spread through my lands and draw closer to the cosmic, conscious bond," replies Mother Nature.

*****

"Our sons, daughters, and wards of the land and all things living, you shall go forth and learn the secrets and language of my heart, but you must always be your brother's keeper and never put ambition above the importance of doing one's duty to your Father Universe and me, Mother Nature.

"Carry out actions to sustain the world and maintain relationship bonds between thy siblings. Be mindful of possessiveness and focus on spiritual discipline, and not the attainment of the elements. The land belongs to no one. It is a gift to man for use to be passed down by the ancestors as a bond between the living and the dead, to be entrusted by each generation for the descendants who would follow until the end of time. One must master intellect through patience and understanding. With these words of decree, I send you forth. Honor thy Mother Earth and thy Father Universe, as we and our love are everlasting, and through our bond, you shall be everlasting!"

Feeling that the children of the earth would often need guidance from higher powers, Father Universe and Mother Nature assigned their celestial offspring to act as guides and advisors by acting to shape the lives and destinies of the earth children. Sun spirit and Moon spirit manifested themselves in physical form as the sun and the moon; they represented the balance of the opposing forces that was the foundation of life. As celestial children, Brother Sun and Sister Moon had powers over the tides and weather of earth, and they had manifested their spirit children, and the spirits lived everywhere and were associated with nature, signifying the close link between the earth children, the land, and the natural world. The celestial children's spirits roles were many, and they each were different in their relationships with the humans. Their responsibility was to control one or more of the forces of nature. There were five essential elemental spirits, which embodied all the things in the natural world, that were birthed out of a union between Father Universe and Mother Nature.

Wind spirit controlled the wind, air, and gas. Wind could shape landforms. Water spirit manipulated and controlled liquid in all forms solid, liquid, and gas. Fire spirit created, destroyed, and controlled fire's flame and heat. Earth spirit controlled the earth; he created, generated, and reshaped rock minerals. Finally, plant spirit manipulated plants, divination through the earth, and earth-based materials.

Many of the spirits were good-natured, but some were mischievous and outright evil spirits. Some spirits were less powerful, but still had an important influence over life, such as the spirits that tide into human daily affairs. The spirits of game and play were in charge of training in some general small crafts, jobs, mixed in with game and play. They dealt with the earth children throughout the years of three years up to twelve years, giving them lessons in primary education, such as arithmetic, teaching tribe dances, storytelling, and identifying the names of different plants, birds, and animals. The spirits of game and play also helped the earth children in bonding with other members of their age group as kin. The spirits of apprenticeship handled the most crucial of ages thirteen to eighteen years; they generally guided the training of all skilled craftsmanship and instructed in all initiation rites for the rites of passage into adulthood. The spirits of adulthood and action dealt with all community and tribal duties and services. This group of tribesmen led the hunt, built affairs in the community, cultivated the fields for planting and all matters concerning home life. These spirits advised the tribesmen from the ages of nineteen years to twenty-eight years. The spirits of the elders remained near to their living descendants to advise and protect them if their relatives remained connected to the cosmic bond, by paying due respect.

In coalition, Brother Sun and Sister Moon combined their energies to move the tides and begin to change the weather. The winds in the valleys and gorges began to pick up in speed, and the air changed from hot and humid to chill and cool. The powerful energies moved across the lands of Mother Nature, and within the next days, the process had created noticeable features of rocks, mountains, hills, rivers, springs, and lakes. Before the spread of the earth children, they were of one telepathic language in the mind and body. The earth children perceived all things plants, animals, rocks, rivers, and weather as possessing a spirit essence or life force. Each object had a spirit essence to either offer help or harm the earth children. Some earth children also manipulated and controlled them through the cosmic bond. Many of the eldest of the earth children had grown their ability to direct or flow within harmony with life energy. Different revelations came about from the climate change and scarcity of food, so some of the sisters and brothers of earth departed from their birth land while most stayed in Ethiopia.

The sons and daughters of the earth traversed from their homeland, populated the world, and settled into new environments—Southwest Asia (the Middle East) Tigris River, Syria, Arabia, Central Asia (Indus Valley) Canaan, Phoenicia, Turkey, India, East Asia (Mediterranean) Asia Manor, and to Europe. Over time, adaptations had developed in skin color and other features that changed because of different climates and environments, which began the first races and classification of the earth children. Earth children did not classify races by color; they identified with people according to their national or tribal names (Ethiopians, Sumerians, Minoans, etc.)

Since the manifestation of Father Universe's energies into physical form, he fathered an energy, out of some type of an asexual process, his first son, Lord Darkness. Lord Darkness, who has control over all things of darkness, was a destructive opposing force and a negative aspect that was linked with Father Universe. He was instantly upset with his father and jealous of the making of the earth children. After eons of isolation in the voids of the dark and nothingness, furious that he was left unrecognized for eons, he vowed to destroy Father Universe and his earth creatures. He stayed patience in his wait, watching intrigued and studying the new creatures as he pondered on a plan to destroy his enemies.

As population increased, the demand for food increased. Life became harder. The earth children had to adapt and transition from hunters and gatherers, with the aid and guidance from the spirit of earth and the spirit of plants. The earth children began to learn how to control the spirit essences of earth and plant. They were taught when the plants grew, where the plants grew best, and how to collect the best plants and seeds to produce better crops during the next planting season. The process of cultivating the soil, planting the seed, tending to the crop until it was ripe and ready to be harvested, and preparing the soil for seeding again dawned the process of farming and agriculture. The same process worked with animals. Controlling the breeding of animals, the earth children was able to turn wolves into loyal hunters(dogs), breed cows, sheep, goats, and chickens. This was the process of domestication, taking something natural (wild) and controlling the breeding to create a new type of organism that is more suitable for one's need. Spoken language started slowly; it developed from a simple symbol system. Eventually symbols were replaced with sounds. The customary rules of life or way of life was wrapped up in the land, the tribe, their relationships, and bond between the cosmic spirits and energies, which helped to explain the powerful natural forces of the cosmos (unforeseen) and offer a way to live in harmony with these forces.

Over centuries, the growth of agriculture contributed to the rise of civilizations. Farming had created a new lifestyle for the earth children. Since farming needed constant attention, this forced the nomadic groups to start living in one place to protect and take care of their crops and fields. These earth children usually settled along rivers and valleys because the soil there was most fertile. In hunter-gatherer tribes, it took the entire day to look for food and water. With farming, earth children could produce enough food for many tribes. This also freed up other earth children to discover and experiment with new things in the world. The world was full of mysteries and changing quickly with the new changes brought by agriculture. Sons and daughters of the earth had time to contemplate and ask questions about the world: How should they act? What is that golden orb that rises, and we take pleasure in its warm rays? The earth children had been laid down the way in which nature's vital force flowed through the cosmic bond of the spirits. The spirit guardians offered answers, mostly in lessons that panned out that an experience or relationship with Father Universe and Mother Nature's life forces, which were the basis for their being, did not have to be expressed in any specific form or image.

Earth's sons and daughters perfected their skills in farming and domestication. Earth children moved from isolated tribes and villages to gather and build cities, nations, and eventually empires. Having trained and studied with a collective knowledge and the understanding of rituals and traditions, each tribe and its tribesmen did its own community and land development planning. With Mother Nature's spirit children training them in their surrounding areas and preferred arts, the earth children became masters of their craft. Farmers were able to select the best grains of Emer and plants of pine corn for the next year coming; craftsmen produced items of charm and beauty, jewelry, pottery, figurines, and statues. With a surplus in food and extra time, tribes started to interact more with one another, because the earth children found that they could not produce all the resources that they needed or wanted. Villages and nations became linked through trade. Long-distance trade had developed to supply communities with raw materials that they needed and goods people wanted, which led to outside merchants. Bartering or gift trade involved the direct exchange of items and services for other items or services. Barter was the trade of goods without the use of money, while gift trades were given in exchange without detailed agreement for immediate or future favors or rewards. As villages interacted and shared resources with one another, this caused a need to keep records and accounts of when they planted seeds or how much they had traded. This process furthered the earth children's skills in developing writing.

There grew to be many different nations, each having its own culture, traditions, history, and folklore. All nations were into learning and teaching one another, not seeing anything to want besides the proper food, shelter, and well-being of the tribe, and had helped the earth children's minds stay clear and focused on their duties to Father Universe and Mother Nature. They lived without greed and ambition of the material world. But soon, the earth children would start thinking in the flesh and not in the spirit. Evolving in its look at the nature of life forces, some earth children wanted to say that Father Universe and Mother Nature indeed had a specific nature. This led to the development of a set of beliefs about why and how earth children were alive.

The existing entity of evil and malice observed, in a fury, the scene of cohesiveness and progression of the earth children. From the voids of darkness, the Lord of Darkness declared, "I am the lord of the nothing—of the darkness. The blackness that is the necessary opposite of being. I am born of the universe's pitches of midnight-black and energies of hate, casted to the voids of eternity to remain in the cosmic darkness, forever forgotten. The thing that troubles me is how easily they are loved and praised, and I am disregarded. This disgusts me!" Looking at the earth creatures, Lord Darkness felt a presence about the earth children that he almost did not notice. They contained a power that he could use to weaken and destroy the universe with. "I must find a way to possess and control that power within them and bring about the end of their creation." Lord Darkness utilized his cosmic energies to create the dark entities of Hate, Confusion, and Chaos.

"Hate, Confusion, Chaos, you must get to earth and bring the souls of the earth children to me. You shall be greatly rewarded. You will become princess in the realm of the dark.

In unison, the dark energies inquired from their master, "Where should we start, our master?"

Lord Darkness responded, "There is only one allure for such disgusting creatures, one means of bait that will never fail—greed!" Lord Darkness instructed his agents in the ways of the earth children and how they were to use the earth's minerals to entice man. They were to intensify the disunity and promote the suspicions and hatred that developed from it and to check all tendencies or movement toward unity among the earth children.

*****

The evolving differences in thinking and the rise of cities and urban centers increased disagreements over land, water, and trade, requiring the need for leaders or council to resolve conflicts. In the chiefless nations, the elders acted as advisory council, and a council meeting was called by senior elders in emergencies. Matters involving members of the same tribe would be settled by the family council, each family having its own elder. Problems could be discussed before any mutually acceptable elder to be resolved. The elder's judgment was not the final judgment of the problem; one could ignore the judgment of their elders at their own risk, for to ignore the elders was like to ignore the community itself. Stated before, there were those members of the community who felt that there was a governing power of the universe that had specific rules in which our minds were to conform, and if you did not watch out, you would go against the grain and be punished.

The emissaries of Lord Darkness—Hate, Confusion, and Chaos—had noticed the potential rift among the nations. They plotted a scheme to capitalize on their opportunity to trick the earth children. One day, a group of earth children were out on a discovery expedition in one of the most inaccessible areas of Ethiopia. While searching the banks of a river, one of the earth children stumbles across a strange-looking rock; it was unlike any other rock that he had seen before. It was shining, glimmering, and reflecting the golden rays from the sun. The golden rock stood out from the other dull-colored rocks. Having the appearance as if it were a piece from the golden orb in the sky, the earth child fell instantly into a trance, caught in the allure of the rock. He called to the other earth children to show what was discovered. They, too, had been hypnotized the instant they had laid eyes on the alluring object. Tiny glimmers of light started to sparkle throughout the valley, and the earth children rushed to collect as many of these little sparkling rocks as they could carry back to the village, to show the community what they discovered.

The group of men were overjoyed with excitement as they entered the village with their mysterious find; the village members eagerly came out to greet the group and to discover their source of excitement. The group of earth children began to pour their findings into a pile in the middle of the village so that the entire community encircled, gazing at the pile of glowing golden rocks, stunned by its beauty and glow. Whispers of chatter emerged throughout the crowd of earth children. They were blinded by the objects' beauty and knew little that the existence of the spirit of true unity and kinship was being threatened. With the discovery of raw materials such as gold, silver, diamonds, and ivory, earth children began to grow their ambition for the things they could not produce by farming and domestication.

Lord Darkness's agents Hate, Confusion, and Chaos had used the earth's minerals (gold, silver, diamonds) of no real nutritional value to entice the earth children's minds. They used the commodities as hosting ports to infiltrate the earth children's minds and bodies, who were weak and unprotected from the cosmic bond, consuming their life essence from within. Siphoning the earth children's essence, Lord Darkness's own powers began to amplify. It was a sensual addiction; the energies flowing increased his growth in power. Lord Darkness witnessed the dawn of the earth children's quest for knowledge and innovation. Knowing that it would be their downfall, he watched with glee as his agents went to work.

Bartering started to involve the precious metals as a medium for exchange in transactions. In the village, when the brewer needed a new brewing pot, he exchanged some beer to the pot maker. The pot maker might need a new roof. The roofer might need a new hat to cover his head from the heat. The hat maker might need a new needle. The blacksmith might need a new coat, and the coat tanner might need a new pot. In these situations, the people might not know one another personally, and they might all need their items at a different time. This led to the production of money; money became the solution to these problems by ensuring that everyone's needs were fulfilled.

Religion grew to be the occasion for the development of art and science; it also inspired the ambition of architecture. Earth children had the same fundamental beliefs. Having come from the same origin, they all believed in the creator of the universe—the Almighty Father, who had his emissaries exist in charge over various aspects of life, each family or clan under the guidance and protection of cosmic energies. There were many ways to express the concept of one supreme spirit. Spiritual bonding was more important than living in the physical; this reflected in their day-to-day way of life.

Tribal chiefs, elders, and kings were leaders representing the earth children and executed their will. Tribe members, not rulers, were the source of power; no one was above the tribe or community.

The role of the elder chief was to offer prayers and sacrifices to the cosmic energies and to be an overseer of the land, seeing to it that all was fairly distributed among all the families. Offerings to appease the cosmic spirits from the tribe members or items produced or earned grew the income of the community. Many clans began to regard their leaders as celestial energies because of some heroes' legendary deeds of great feats, being exaggerated over time, or because of others who have lived the standard of important values. The mysteries of the cosmos had such a strong influence on the lives of the earth children that some of the craftier leaders noticed that the beliefs in the cosmos made the earth children obedient and submissive.

Civilization became the result of the needs of cultivating and farming; all the first cities began in the great river valleys. First, in Mesopotamia, earth children settled along the Tigris and Euphrates, in the upper and lower Egypt along the Nile. Second, the Indus River civilization on the subcontinent of India, and then the small farming communities, cultivating the terraces of the Yellow River. With the fast rise of trade and expansions of crafts such as agriculture, industrial and building developments, science, arts, religion, mining, and shipbuilding, religion had become the starting point of power, both economic and political. The growth of the first great cities with monumental architecture began a new era. One of the most important outcomes was the change in the traditional role of the elder chief—as the chief representative of the people before Father Universe. The elder chief was now changed and viewed as the lieutenant of God on earth. The chief or king could assume powers now, which were once checked and kept in balance by tribe members, without challenge. Industrial pursuits, particularly mining, began to overshadow the earth children's duties of nurturing and perfecting his spiritual craft. The first earth children of learning—priests, scribes, historians, and others were in the most prominent position to attain power. Priests had promoted the evolution of the idea of the chief's role as the medium with the ancestor and cosmic energies to the idea of the leader's blood ties to the cosmic energies, therefore making the chief divine, dawn of God of man. Architecture had brought astonishing buildings and monuments (Ziggurat of Ur, Pyramid of Djoser) that were meant to impress the gods and to divide the ruling classes from the common tribe members, and to exaggerate the divine characteristics of the ruler. This meant that each king would try to outdo the previous king in building a bigger and more glamorous temple or massive burial structure.

The success of trade in ancient times, on both sides of the Red Sea between Africa and Arabia, meant power, control of trade posts, and control of key positions within the nation. Man had strengthened his political and economic influence over the tribes' culture, and civilization spread. As powers began to imperialize the world, the old ways became under threat.

Earth children had established powerful governments and built empires that extended in all directions, both in Ethiopia and Mesopotamia. The wealth was in the hands of the new elite—priests, kings, soldiers, and bureaucracies. The evolving differences in the changing systems grew into much jealousy and trade rivalry among alliances that had maintained international commerce in multitudes of raw materials with the eastern and western earth children. Political power was predicated on the possession of gold and raw materials. The culturally advanced felt superior to the tribes of the old ways and enslaved many of these tribes; territorial expansion was the idea of nations as one brotherhood. The exotic items traded from Ethiopia and Egypt sparked the curiosity of the other earth nations, with its elephants, ivories, gold, diamonds, and other resources. Lost in the competition of building and innovation, they launched wars against one another in their efforts to build empires greater than any that had existed. Kings and leaders sought to convert to their new religion or way of life. There were earth children who were adamant and resistant to the changes. The high regard and respect that rulers held for tribe members turned into enmity, and instead of being seen as allies, they looked upon them as competitors. Therefore, they turned against the members of the tribe and became their tormentors. Men's throats were cut from ear to ear; rulers became religious extremist. Their patience had been pushed to its limits; rulers had become determined to spread his religion, if not by persuasion, then by force of the sword. For example, one thousand people were gathered in a village marketplace and given the ultimatum of converting to man's new religion or face the sword. The earth children did not hesitate in their choice that of being free in death rather than being alive as a slave. The ruler executed the men and sold the women into slavery. The strength derived from their conquests of their earthly brothers and sisters and their wealth had led them to believe that they were the superior man and rightful rulers of earth. At this point of civilization, a conflict of viewpoints between those who represented the masters of the "world" and those who rebelled against those who oppressed their brothers and sisters of the earth had caused many successive wars to be fought among one another.

CHAPTER 4

Our Father, who art in heaven, hallowed be thy name. Thy kingdom comes. Thy will be done, on earth as it is in heaven. Give us this day our daily bread. And forgive us our trespasses, as we forgive those who trespass against us. And lead us not into temptation but deliver us from evil for thine is the kingdom and the power and the glory, forever and ever. Amen.

I pledge allegiance to the flag of the United States of America and to the republic for which it stands, one nation under God, indivisible, with liberty and justice for all.

A loud crackling sound of a school's loudspeaker.

"Good morning. It's Friday February 24, 2006. I am Andrew Goldman."

"And I am Nina Barber."

"And we are your hosts of the CHHS morning news and announcements!"

> GOLDMAN: "Attention all students, Monday February 27th, will be a testing day, students will be either taking the PSAT or the underclassmen placement exam. Some classes will be relocated due to testing, please check the 'Weekly Messages Bulletin' in the main halls for Monday's class relocations. Relocations are also posted inside of the cafeteria and gymnasium on Monday morning. Testing will be ongoing in the senior hall, so please be quiet during class changes, we would like to try to be less disruptive as possible."

BARBER: Heuman High will be hosting its first Come Read with Me event with the seniors and juniors, Saturday March 4 from two to six p.m. Students of all grades will be able to come out and help read to children of the community. To volunteer, sign up, and or donate we will have more information coming to you soon. Students, those who missed the February 2 Student Government Career Day, the next trip will be on March 5, all paperwork and forms have been transferred.

GOLDMAN: In sports, anyone interested in wrestling, please come by Coach Rodin's room in B-25 before the end of next week. Practice begins on Monday, March 5, meeting in Coach Rodin's room at 3:30 p.m. Good luck to our Lady Raiders softball team, as they travel to Boca today for round 2 of the FHSAA triple-A softball tournament. Best wishes sent to our volleyball team that plays here, Saturday at one, kicking off their run in the state tournament. Finally, we, I, would like to congratulate the Raiders boys' varsity basketball team, for a great season and commend them in their efforts in last night's 76 to 79 season-ending loss. Great job guys, keep your heads up!

BARBER: And now for your CHHS news weather report, today's high will be a high of eighty-one degrees with a low of sixty-five degrees and a 30 percent chance of rain today. Today in history, 1980 US ice hockey team clinches gold medal with a 4–2 win over Finland at the Lake Placid Winter Olympics, coming after a 4–3 miracle-on-ice victory against favorite Soviet Union.

GOLDMAN: Birthdays! Happy birthday to Lauren Burke, Maria Paulk, and Katlyn Morris. From the CHHS NEWS team, Happy birthday to you! We hope that you have a fabulous Friday and as always, go, Raiders!"

*****

48

"OK, is it time to go yet? I have just about had enough of today already," says Ronin to Paul while they sit and wait for Mrs. Henderson, their homeroom teacher, to call attendance and make her morning remarks.

"I can see that you are in your slump about the loss, but I am sure by the end of the night, we should have you cheered up a bit and your mind off the game," Paul exclaims in his attempt to boost up Ronin's spirit. Ronin is clearly not feeling as optimistic as his friend about his prediction, with him thinking that the last place he wants to be was in a crowd of peers.

"Good morning, class!" Mrs. Henderson is standing at her podium and greeting the class while opening her lesson's planning book, then proceeds to announce names. "Ambrose, Anderson, Andrews, Banks, Barker. The students quietly raise their hands, acknowledging the instructor as she rolls through her attendance sheet.

Paul is amusingly making faces across the room at another female classmate. Meanwhile, Ronin attempts to clear his mind about his next class—history, he has to recite the famous "Friends, Romans, countrymen, lend me your ears" speech spoken by Mark Antony in the play *Julius Caesar* written by William Shakespeare. He had been working half-heartedly on memorizing the address, but the subject of Roman history just seems dull and dry to him; in fact, pretty much all history seems boring and uninteresting to Ronin. There are few events in history that piques his interests, and those periods are up to and after the Emancipation era. Most of that just makes him feel angry, upset, and helpless. He feels it serves him better to not keep his interests in the history of his people being dehumanized and enslaved. History is more Iesha's thing; Ronin just has her help him out from time to time. The sciences are where Ronin's interests lie—biology, environmental science, astrology, you name it.

Completing her call of attendance, Mrs. Henderson continues in her deliverance of current events. "First, I would like to say, good job and great season to the guys on the basketball team. You guys had a fine season, and you really put forth a great effort last night," she begins with a round of applause, and the class joins along. Ronin and Paul, the only members of the team in the class, gives their bashful appreciation. "Now onto the next order of business. Juniors, if you have not already done so, please turn in your student résumé. Ms. Hampton cannot start recommendation for courses until she receives your student résumé. Next week, on Tuesday and Wednesday, is the Juniors' My Plan Day. Be sure you are collecting and preparing information needed to complete your college-prep applications. The county's canned food drive is next Monday and will proceed for the next two weeks in your homeroom period. The drive benefits the PBC Food Bank, which gives food and aid to families in need across Providencia County. Our goal is for every student to bring in three to four cans. Prizes will be given each week for the top classes that bring in the most cans. Every class that brings in at least seventy cans will get a snack prize the following Friday. This wraps it up as far as upcoming events are concerned, so I bid you all a great Friday and a safe weekend as the bell should be ringing shortly within the next five minutes or so. You can now use the remaining time to gather your belongings for your day's classes. Have a great weekend and see you guys next week on Monday." Mrs. Henderson takes her leave from the podium to return to her desk, to prepare herself for the day ahead.

Several students remain in their seats, engaging in causal chatter. Some students head to their lockers within the classroom, positioned along a wall opposite the instructor's desk. Ronin and Paul are in discussion, with Paul having his continuous rant about the importance of making an impact in the high school hierarchy of popularity.

"I hate to cut you off," interrupts Ronin, "but I need to grab my stuff from my locker. Honestly, I just need to focus on reciting Julius Caesar."

"Oh yeah, you have to do that today?" inquires Paul. "I have to go on Wednesday. I almost forgot about that. Thanks for the reminder!"

"No problem. I have been only talking to you about my painful progress of getting through the play for the past week and a half," says Ronin.

"It just slipped my mind. As a matter of fact, there is my line to get Chelsea to come study with me later. You go handle your business at your locker, I'm going to go set up this study session," exclaims Paul as he slides out of his seat to speak with his female classmate.

Ronin heads from his seat and moves along toward his locker, walking down the narrow aisles of desk and traversing over and around lingering legs and feet. During his display of high kneeing through the extremities of his fellow classmates, Ronin accidently bumps into another classmate, and obviously, not the most pleasant of mates from the reaction—Quentin Gary.

"Excuse me, Quentin, didn't mean to bump into you," expresses Ronin.

Quentin immediately spins around and shoves Ronin. "I see why the help didn't get it done last night. We picked the clumsy niggers!" He then turns and continues at his locker. Ronin is taken back and in a bit of shock at what had just transpired that he was not sure on how to react or respond to what occurred. He is not expecting an altercation, all he's thinking is, *Years later after segregation, the ruling classes of the world had not changed their real attitude toward people of color and that his race was still in the same position.* Ronin wants to be absent of his mind and go King Kong on Quentin. At the same time, Ronin knows that will lead him straight into administration involvement and he does not want to stress his mother out any more than she had been in her battles against bills and debts. And crazy as it may seem, Ronin even thought to himself that some parts of what his classmate had said are true. Inside his heart, darkness is starting to grow, which led his anger to turn into hate.

Confused and angry all at the same time, Ronin is stuck in the midst of his thoughts. Ronin, in a trance, continues to gather his belongings from his locker. He has to input the combination code three times before he is able to open his lock to retrieve his books and notepads, frustrated with his weak self-consciousness and being in a position where others' views affect him. Outsiders view of disgust cannot compare with his own disgust of himself.

The bell sounds, releasing homeroom period. Students gather their belongings and begin to exit the classroom.

Ronin and Paul meet up in the hallway.

"Can you believe what this fat fuck just said to me?" says Ronin.

"What's up? What are you talking about?" replies Paul.

"Fucking Quentin," answers Ronin. "I'm walking to my locker, and I accidently bumped into him. I said 'Excuse me.' The fucker turned around and shoved me and said, 'I see why the help couldn't get it done last night, and that they had to choose better niggers!'"

"And he is still on his way to class?" says Paul. "The old Ronin would have jumped on Quentin in an instance. You sure aren't feeling well."

When they were younger, before basketball got serious to him, Ronin had anger issues. He was quick to get angry and would fight.

"Not even that, it was a petty situation. I was caught off guard by it. I was not expecting the declaration of a personal war over unintentionally bumping into someone," states Ronin.

"Well, what do you expect from the Sugarcane Prince?" replies Paul.

Quentin's great-grandfather founded one of the most successful sugarcane companies in South Florida and the business had established a strong line of power. Quentin's father has been heading the company for the past fifteen years.

"He comes from a line of 'Mr. Big House on the Hills' and pass judgment on those who disrupt their peace. You just have to kind of steer clear of him," exclaims Paul.

"I guess that just goes to show us that we still have to be on our toes at all times and not be so naive falling into the illusion that our world is perfect and problems of race do not exist," says Ronin.

"It sure would have been funny to see you put Quentin on his ass, for real," Paul jokingly adds.

"Yeah, sure would have felt a lot better than doing nothing," says Ronin.

The pair makes their way through the busy corridor, then gives each their routine "see you later," sending each other off: Ronin to history and Paul to Spanish.

*****

Ronin is sitting in a classroom decorated with flags of nations that joined the United Nations. The flags dangled vertically, hanging from the classroom ceiling, arranged in rows and columns. Ronin stares into space, tuning out Mr. Lupin, his history teacher, as he goes through his introductory to class, giving his best Ben Stein impersonation in the scene from *Ferris Bueller's Day Off.* Ronin cannot help but question the sake of his dignity and masculinity by not taking a good whack at Quentin in the jaw; it has made him feel like a coward by not taking a stand.

Mr. Lupin explains to the class that they would spend the first forty-five minutes of class viewing a documentary on ancient Rome civilization and that they would spend the remaining time in class giving their oral examinations, which the class gladly appreciated the extra time to review Antony's speech.

"Rome began as a small village, in central Italy along the Tiber River. Over the coming centuries, it expanded its empire, which extended from the North Atlantic to the Persian Gulf," spoke the narrator of the documentary.

Ronin is attempting to clear his head and focus on Antony's address. "Friends, Romans, countrymen, lend me your ears. I came here to bury Caesar, not to praise him," recites Ronin in his review session. But he cannot escape from wandering off in his thoughts, thinking about what was said by his classmate. He resumes watching the documentary., thinking, *In ancient times, for an insult like that, he would have gladly challenged his nemesis to a duel to the death in the name of his honor and pride.* Ronin imagines himself as a gladiator battling in the great colosseums, defying death for glory. Slipping further into his fantasies, he sees himself as a courageous samurai scrapping in the feudal era exhibiting the spirits of "no surrender and no retreat." Ronin feels that the heritages of these cultures would have never accepted any type of insults on their pride and honor; that also has made him feel shameful about not contesting his classmate. It is bad enough not hearing of many historical events in which his culture achieved something great without the aid of outside influences, appeasing or appealing to some outside forces. This has just made him feel overwhelmed and made it seem impossible for his spirit to escape the feeling of eternal subservience. Ronin realizes that, that situation has taken more effect on him than the game had. It is a must that he breaks out of that feeling of subjugation.

"By the fourth century after a reign of over a millennia, the Roman Empire declined. Internal factors such as political corruption, economic crises, and class conflicts led to the fall of the empire from within. Invasion and other military threats caused it to fall externally. Many lessons can be learned from Rome's rich history of dominating rivalries, incorporating various cultures, and adapting its systems to meet the needs of its people," concludes the narrator of the film, as the documentary's score blares through the classroom.

"Let's hope that warmed you guys up and put you in the spirits of performing and giving the best Mark Antony impressions," says Mr. Lupin, making his way to turn the classroom lights back on. "Not everyone jumps for joy. I must ask you to contain all that enthusiasm I feel oozing from your pores!" Mr. Lupin comments, amusingly toying with his student's emotions as he observes the beads of sweat coming from some of his students. "So who's up first at the chopping block?" teases Mr. Lupin. "I figured that instead of going down the list in alphabetical order, I would allow those with courage the opportunity to volunteer in presenting first."

Most students in the room are wearing blank faces, some shying away, shooting aimless stares across the room at one another, making all attempts to avoid eye contact with their instructor.

"Let's not all jump at once," speaks Mr. Lupin, daring one of his students to take the first leap. Mr. Lupin takes a moment while entertaining the symphony of the crickets and confused faces. "Come on, is there not a brave soul out there willing to face the gallows?" taunts Mr. Lupin in this theatrical expression. "Well, I guess that leaves me no choice but to take up the mundane task of calling those up to the guillotine."

In that moment, Ronin suddenly feels he has nothing to lose, and he becomes compelled to take up the challenge of his instructor, so he raises his hand. "Mr. Lupin," calls out Ronin, "I'm ready to go."

"Ah, Sir Ronin," calls out Mr. Lupin in excitement, "how noble of you to be the first to sacrifice yourself and tests your loins, giving confidence in your preparation!"

Ronin isn't sure on how confident he is, but he has been preparing, and he feels that if he has to go, he might as well get it done and over with. The walk from his seat to the podium feels like walking the Green Mile, the feeling and pressure of being the first to do something is a weight that Ronin will not take for granted. Anxiously standing in front of his classmates, Ronin glances across the room, takes a breath to gather his composure, and he stares into the flags dangling from the ceiling, avoiding his audiences' eyes. Ronin begins to deliver his speech from the play.

> Friends, Romans, countrymen, lend me your ears; I come to bury Caesar, not to praise him. The evil that men do lives after them; The good is oft interred with their bones; So let it be with Caesar. The noble Brutus Hath told you Caesar was ambitious: If it were so, it was a grievous fault; And grievously hath Caesar answer'd it. Here, under leave of Brutus and the rest—For Brutus is an honourable man; So are they all, all honourable men—Come I to speak in Caesar's funeral. He was my friend, faithful and just to me: But Brutus says he was ambitious; And Brutus is an honourable man. He hath brought many captives home to Rome. Whose ransoms did the general coffers fill: Did this in Caesar seem ambitious? When that the poor have cried, Caesar hath wept: Ambition should be made of sterner stuff: Yet Brutus says he was ambitious; And Brutus is an honourable man. You all did see that on the Lupercal I thrice presented him a kingly crown, Which he did thrice refuse: was this ambition? Yet Brutus says he was ambitious; And, sure he is an honourable man. I speak not

to disprove what Brutus spoke, But here I am to speak what I do know. You all did love him once not without cause: What cause withholds you than to mourn for him? O judgement! Thou art fled to brutish beasts, And men have lost their reason. Bear with me; My heart is in the coffin there with Caesar, And I must pause till it come back to me.

Clap, clap, clap.

"Bravo!" shouts Mr. Lupin, giving praise. "That could not have been a better eulogy if it were spoken by Mark Antony himself."

For a moment, Ronin feels somewhat relieved. Taking his seat, he knows that will only last for a short time.

The remainder of Ronin's day at school goes by pretty stress-free and uneventful. In literature, he catches himself struggling to keep himself awake through the reading of *Antigone*, a Greek tragedy written by Sophocles about a heroine who dies because of her loyalty to her family and beliefs in the gods. During lunch period, he barely survives the waves of debate by the guys on the team about who did and who did not maintain responsibilities in the loss of last night's contest. Sitting throughout biology is just a session of Ronin passively participating. Mrs. Wigley, his instructor, asks if he is feeling well because he is usually one of the most active students during class. By the time he makes it to algebra II, Ronin is worn down from the day and is more than ready to be done with school for the week. The concluding bells, ending the week's school session, is music to his ears. Ronin can think of nothing more than avoiding all conversations and making a beeline straight for his bus stop, but before that can happen, he has a few tasks to get done on campus.

As a part of the scholarship and work-study program, Ronin works by doing janitorial and landscaping services on school grounds, which is supervised by the school's head custodian, Mr. Sargent. Ronin does anything from pressure-cleaning the sidewalks and buildings to sanding and repriming doors or planting and watering baby foxtail palms. The bulk of Ronin's earnings goes toward tuition, books, and uniforms; leaving the remainder as more than enough pocket change for him to get by on and put some up as shoebox money, as he likes to call it. But majority of the time, by the end of practice, he only has to vacuum the hallways and classrooms and empty out the rooms' trash cans.

Now that season has ended and there is no practice, Ronin is thinking of killing time, to let the school clear out of its students, by going to the weight room to get a workout done. Coach Donald, the head football coach and PE instructor, is always in the mood to persuade Ronin to come out and play some spring football. Ronin has enjoyed hearing the coach in his enthusiastic sales pitch during his class.

"Ronin, I could use you as a good pass rusher! I'm just telling you, son, you have the prototype to be a great defensive end!" he would say.

A good pep talk and pump should let his mind escape for a while. Before Ronin arrives at his solitary place, he is intercepted by his friend Paul and teammate Erik, or EA. They want to give him the rundown of that night's planned agenda.

"Woo! Thank God for the weekend!" sings Paul in a cheerful and excited voice as he found Ronin among their hyper schoolmates. "Tonight, it is going down! There's going to be so many females out there tonight," says Paul.

"So many females!" Erik repeats Paul's statement, confirming his approval of the night's expectations.

"The two partners in crime seem to be ready for this evening's round of activities," says Ronin, teasing the pair.

"We most definitely are! The only thing we need to do is hit the mall for some fresh new outfits and touch down at the barber shop," explains Paul.

"We just came to see if you wanted to roll with us," asks Erik.

"Had to check and see if the homey wanted to go!" states Paul.

"You guys know I'm always down to ride, but actually, I think I am going to hit the weight room," replies Ronin. "I'm looking for something right now, guys, and I do not think I can find it at the mall. I have to go and let out some of this steam, and plus, I still have clean-up duties before I can call it quits."

"I hear ya, man, but I hope you are not letting last night or what happened this morning stress you out, bro!"

"What happened this morning?" asks Erik.

"Nothing, man," replies Paul. Making lite of the Quentin subject.

"But we are going to let this one slide for now, but by the time night comes around, you Ronin should be ready to have a good time and relax with us boys," proclaims Paul.

"I think I can try to manage that," answers Ronin.

"We are going to get out of here and get into some action. Hit me up later when you get to the crib, so we can set up a time to come through and scoop you up," says Paul as he gives Ronin a handshake. Erik follows his lead and does the same as well.

"Later!" Erik calls out as he and Paul depart through the halls, making conversation with others in the student body.

Through the halls and past the school's courtyard, Ronin makes his way toward the school weight room. As he walks, Ronin is carefully thinking of a few exercises he wants to go through within the next forty-five minutes to an hour.

"I can start off with a light stretch session, get some push-ups in. Maybe do some squats, get some arm exercises going, and I think that should do it," Ronin tells himself. He swings by the school locker room, located on the back end of the gymnasium to change into his workout attire, then crossing the parking lot to the weight room.

Bump, bump, bump!

Ronin can hear the sound of techno music playing inside the weight room. When he enters the building, the first-person Ronin spots is Coach Donald, blasting a set out on the latissimus dorsi pull-down machine, with a few of his varsity players waiting in line to get their turn in sets. Coach Donald completes his set and rises from the exercise machine with a howl.

"Woo, that pump!" Coach Donald shouts, swinging his arms across his body as if to loosen them up. Then he notices Ronin coming into the room. "Drummond! What's up?" greets Coach Donald. "You came in to get some of this good work today?"

"Hey, Coach. Yeah, I came to get a good sweat in before the weekend," replies Ronin.

"Good, good and now that you are in here, maybe I can convince you to come out this spring!" Coach Donald chuckles.

"I don't know. Maybe after last night, who knows. I just might need to bang some heads," says Ronin.

"That's what I'd like to hear! So what you are working today?" asks Coach Donald.

Ronin gives him a quick overview of his routine of calisthenics and auxiliary exercises.

"Seems like you got it all covered for today," says Coach Donald. "Go ahead and get to business." He gives a pat to Ronin on his shoulders, returning to his place among the line of players.

"All right, Coach. I will catch up to you later!" replies Ronin.

Finding himself a vacant corner in the weight room, Ronin begins stretching, and in a childish manner, he mocks the actions of his classmate to himself.

"I see why the help didn't get it done! I'll show you help," Ronin says to himself. He aims to use the thinking of his small-minded classmate as fuel to his motivation during his workout session. Ronin plugs his headphones into his ear and blasts through his playlist. Pondering, Ronin is thinking of how most of all the men he knows from birth were made to feel like they were useless. He is determined to find value in his own uniqueness and give it to the world.

Ronin rips through his routine, pushing himself to his limits. Five sets of twenty squats, three sets of sixty calf raises, finishing off his leg workout with a few rounds of leg extensions. Now walking around the weight room like a newborn baby giraffe, Ronin has a good fifteen minutes to spare, so he decides to finish his workout with super sets (repetition of exercises performed one after another) of triceps extensions and bicep curls. Ronin's body is tight and pumped with blood flowing through is veins. He feels refreshed as he walks out of the school's weight room. Ronin feels that he can conquer the world!

Now he just needed to finish with his work responsibilities, and then he is free to enjoy his weekend. Ronin heads in the direction of the custodians' office. As he strides, Ronin thinks of his sister, Iesha. He is thinking about how Iesha's eight hours went and if she had any worthwhile encounters throughout her day. He sure cannot wait to tell her about his eventful day. When he gets to the custodian's office, the head custodian, Mr. Sargent and his assistant Chris are in the middle of discussion. From the sounds of it, they are speaking about the plans for next week's event setup.

"There he is," salutes Mr. Sargent as Ronin comes into the room. "Man, what happened last night?" he asks.

Besides the cafeteria workers, Mr. Sargent and his assistants, Chris and Frank, are the only African American staff at the school, so they always relate to the young athletes at the school. They are never short on words of encouragement, always prepared to comment on the games, or they are not too far around the corner to give a good, stern look of disapproval to keep the guys focused and on track.

"Man, I don't know. That first half killed us," replies Ronin. "It was like we were all shaken up and nervous. We were all out of control, turning the ball over and making careless mistakes. We settled down the second half and got it together, ended up going on a run of our own. But that twenty-five-point lead we gave up in the first proved to be too great to overcome," explains Ronin.

"Well, young buck, at least ya'll didn't just lay down. Ya'll went as hard as ya'll could. All right, I'm going to go and finish getting this paint set up in the locker rooms," says Chris, Mr. Sargent's lead assistant, as he hurries out of the office, with his kneepads and paintbrushes in hand.

"Later, Chris," says Ronin, proceeding to the custodian supply closet.

"You and the fellas are aching at the moment. Got to be more careful early in the game," exclaims Mr. Sargent.

"Yeah, until next year," huffs Ronin, grabbing a pair of latex gloves and trash can liners to dress the building's garbage cans.

"You boys had one hell of a season to remember. Keep your head up. Better prepare for the trip up the mountain next season. Never hang your head, son!" says Mr. Sargent, attempting to keep a fire lit within his young pupil's spirit.

"Thanks, Mr. Sargent, I'm sure I will be motivated this off-season," answer's Ronin.

"Maybe after the weekend you will be in better spirits. And on that note, assistant principal Bachman caught a student defacing a desk during his detention session with a wad of bubble gum. He radioed and asked me to bring over some cleaning supplies so that the student could get on cleanup detail. Good news for you is that you only have the upstairs and downstairs of this building to clear out today," explains the chief custodian, grabbing his key ring and walkie talkie from his desk. "Just lock it up when you leave out of here, and if I don't see you before you are done, have a good weekend!" Then the head custodian slips out of the office doors.

"Later, Mr. Sargent, have a good weekend," says Ronin.

Hearing about some of the incidents that Mr. Sargent and the crew had dealt with on a day-to-day basis makes Ronin appreciate the lessons on improving the resolve in his character. Proceeding to his duties, Ronin notices the time on the clock: 3:45 p.m.

I have about an hour and twenty minutes before the bus is scheduled to come, thinks Ronin.

Now that the halls are empty of students and he has been assigned to cleaning one building today, he plans to make a smooth getaway. Diving back into the utilities closet, Ronin grabs one of the vacuum backpacks and straps the pack's harness. Secretly Ronin enjoys strapping into the equipment, and many times, when idling in time or just amusing himself, he would pretend that he was one of the Ghost Busters from out of the 1980s movies, blasting demon spirits with plasma rays. For an instance there, Ronin begins to think that even though they had ended their season last night and that he had an encounter with his socially challenged classmate, today's school day had ended reasonably OK.

Streaking up and down the main hallways entering classrooms and offices of the high school building, Ronin diligently vacuums the carpets and empties the trash cans and recycle bins. This afternoon's work session is light work. Cleaning is a breeze. The upper level has no more than a few scraps of crumpled paper and torn pieces of candy wrappers scattered on its floor. After hours, this area is less of a student social at dismal. Progressing though the second floor's corridors working in a zone from the rhythm of music, Ronin approaches the doors of Mrs. Henderson's homeroom class. Ronin peers at number 201 on the door and instantly gives thought back to the incident that morning. The drama replays in his head, a thought his memory bank just would not let go. There is just something inside Ronin nagging him about not retaliating and taking a stand against Quentin. He feels that his classmate has a definite problem with his attitude, and it most definitely needs to be checked.

While vacuuming his homeroom's floors, Ronin filters through his mind the perfect idea of getting back at Quentin. He knows that outside that instance, Quentin will never get into a physical altercation with him. Quentin has the reputation of letting Daddy's power work for him.

"Five minutes alone in the locker room. I'd scrub the floor with him," he says those words to himself and instantly is upset with himself for not making his move, giving signs of a coward. "Should have started and finished the fight!" he shouts and clenches his fist, pounding the top of a desk.

Suddenly, a sharp, stinging pain fires off within the fingertips of Ronin. "Arrgghh!" shouts Ronin in pain. The nerves in the tips of his fingers feels as if they had just exploded and set fire. The tips of his phalanges take on the worst case of Charlie Horse that he has ever taken on. After a few seconds of intense pain, which had seemed like it lasted a lifetime, the muscle spasms shooting from the tips of his fingers to his forearms has subsided.

"Damn it, need to eat more bananas. Potassium must be low, didn't hydrate enough, or something," he exclaims to himself. He gathers his equilibrium and then sits on top of one of the desks for second. Ronin wipes the beads of sweat from his forehead. "Man, cramps in the fingers hurt. Got both my arms numb!"

The clock strikes 4:35 p.m. Ronin notices the time. His bus is scheduled to arrive at 5:15 p.m., so he continues vacuuming the remaining aisles. He then completes the final row in the room, which so happens to be the aisle as the lockers. Glancing at the lockers, he sees something interesting. Ronin sees that the padlock on Quentin's locker has not been securely snapped shut. The excitement from his discovery sends his emotions in a frenzy. Overwhelmed with the thought of not putting up any resistance to the verbal assault of his classmate, he gives in to his temptations.

It is practically like an invitation, he says in his mind. It is not like he is going into a bank; he is only interested in getting a little revenge and showing someone, you cannot talk to people anyway and get away with it.

Ronin swipes Quentin's locker clear of all its belongings—math, biology, and music appreciation textbooks; a few notepads; and loose pieces of paper. Books in hand, Ronin slips the padlock back in place, but this time, he snaps the lock closed and exits smoothly out of the classroom. Ronin heads directly toward his mobile trash can and tosses the textbooks and notepads into the can. In his state of euphoria from this meager moment of redemption, Ronin is on could nine, entranced in his plot of vengeance. He feels that this is just a little justice for the unwarranted assault. Ronin grins to himself, thinking he just pulled the perfect revenge ploy, and has the weekend before anyone learns what's done to Quentin's locker.

"Yeah, this weekend maybe OK," says Ronin as he places the equipment back into the utilities closet. After retrieving his bag, Ronin exits the school grounds, closing out another week in the chapters of the high school soap opera. He then begins his jog to his bus stop to head home. Ronin is looking forward to getting home to catch up with his sister on their day; he even begins to look forward to meeting up with the guys later that evening too. He makes it to the bus stop at 5:10 p.m., and he did not have to count that many cars after arriving at the bus stop. Like clockwork, the bus approaches to make its journey back across town.

CHAPTER 5

AFTER ABOUT FORTY-FIVE MINUTES THROUGH South Florida's stop-and-go five-o'clock traffic, Ronin dozes off during most of the trip, listening to his playlist of movie scores. He is a frequent visionary of epic tales and adventures, comparing his life to fantasy films. The bus pulls up to Ronin's stop, just as the sun has begun its descent behind the sky's horizon, bringing the time of dusk. Fatigued, he shuffles off the bus, his legs now feels tight, his arms soar and aching.

"Looks like today kicked your butt!" Ronin hears as he disembarks from the bus.

"Lo and behold," he responds, "my little sister, never missing a beat." Ronin is not surprised seeing that the first face that he sees after stepping off the bus is that of his baby sister. Iesha patiently waits at the bus stop for the arrival of her older brother, standing in hand with a text of *Their Eyes Were Watching God*, written by Zora Neale Hurston. "Don't tell me, you missed me that much today?" he teases his sister.

"I like you, but not that much. I just had to make sure you didn't get lost on the way home. It's been a pretty long day, and you like to wander so!" she fires back. The two siblings lock eyes, and they begin to chuckle at each other; continuing their never-ending tease war.

"So what's up? Today kick your butt like my day?" asks Ronin, with him knowing Iesha must be anxious to trade stories about today's events. She is rarely outside the house without him.

"Besides surviving the predation from the packs of jackals, hyenas, and other sorts of scavengers, it was a rather OK day," says Iesha. "I even met a couple of associates today. They were asking about starting a study group."

"What? Can I believe my ears? Did you just say you made some friends? It was bound to happen sooner or later. My sister has been bitten by the social bug," he taunts. Ronin is used to his antisocial little sister running behind his tail always.

"Mind you, I said associates, just a trial-and-error period. Cashback guarantee upon return," Iesha responds. The pair continues to giggle and set about their walk home. "They even invited me to a party tonight! At first, I was against it, but they kept at it, insisting that I come out. So now I am thinking officially. I am in high school, and I am technically caught up on all my assignments, so I'm like, why not go? Wanted to see what you had planned for tonight," Iesha explains.

"I still cannot believe my ears. I am getting a Friday night's itinerary rundown from my antisocial kid sister who's gone social. But small world, I got an invite to the same party. Today continues to be one of those Alice-tumbling-down-the-rabbit-hole type of days. Crazy thing about it, Shakespeare was not the highlight of my day. And I did not mean that in a bad way because I did surprisingly well on it!" says Ronin, explaining to Iesha. He also goes on to tell her about his two altercations in the day—starting with his bus ride to school and then explaining the verbal attack from his jerk classmate in homeroom.

"Seems like you have had it out for some trouble after last night's loss," says Iesha in a comforting tone, absorbing the information from Ronin.

He further explains how the situation from homeroom had thrown him off and had him like a deer stuck in the headlights. Acquainted with the short temper of Ronin, Iesha is surprised at her brother's lack of aggression. Ronin does not go out of his way to make trouble, but he sure is not keen on backing down once provoked either. But in the end, she is grateful for the showing of some self-control from Ronin. The fewer street brawl stories, the better. But Ronin being Ronin assures his little sister that an opportunity at some form of revenge and attaining some dignity presented itself to him after school. Not being the biggest fan of her brother's thoughtless act of revenge, Iesha does not hesitate to give lecture to her brother on his deed and of the possibilities of the long-run effects. In many situations, Iesha sounds more like the elder sibling. At the end of it, Iesha knows her brother, and something in his spirit just never backs down from things that never let him alone. Ronin listens to the scolding from his little sister, not giving much argument or resistance to Iesha's critique. Ronin does not know what tomorrow or what next week will bring, and he really does not care, but in that moment, he feels justified about his stand of personal justice.

There is a tranquil feeling that evening in the neighborhood, even though the neighborhood looks gritty with apartment buildings with chipped paint and lined with rented homes that had overgrown lawns. The weather is not too humid; there is a nice, cool breeze blowing, and the activity on the block is not intense. The guys on the block, who are having their routine evening hangout, are not roused up. They stroll past the community park, witnessing a group of boys from the neighborhood playing a game of pick-up basketball, making comments, and discussing further their ideas on the night's upcoming events.

*****

Unbeknownst to the siblings, who are indulged with their time in conversation, an insidious energy progresses to finalize its scheme to strengthen the imbalance and the disturbance of Mother Earth's spirit.

"Lord Chaos! Lord Destruction! Come, talk with me," a cold and callus voice commands over an intercom.

"Yes, sire," answers two dark figures, heading to step through the doors of a top-level executive building.

"Yes, my master, what is it that you would like to discuss with us?" inquires the dark energy of Lord Chaos, proud and loyal, ready to serve at his master's request.

"Thousands of years have gone on in this realm of time since the beginning of my campaign against, Father Universe and his consort Mother Earth. Since the creation of their so-called love children— the humans—I have expressed loathing for them. It comes as a surprise to me to almost say that I have come to love that which I have hated. But as the earth children have come to say, 'It is a thin twine between love and hate.' Could you have imagined it? The very creatures that I have established this hate and rage against are the exact instruments that will deal the final blows in undermining my father's kingdom, escalating wars of colonization, solidifying the institutions of religion, industrialism, and capitalism. Over time, my father's precious earth children's praise and allegiance to my cause far outweighs their love for him or their Mother Earth. But as the humans also say, 'Almost does not count,' and from previous experiences, I have come to learn not to get ahead of myself. Always close to a point of satisfaction and then a blistering blunder comes tumbling down from the mountains to interrupt the party. Somehow these pests of beings find some spirit of fight and produce some gallant effort of hope in spoiling my plans. So tell me what the reports are on seeking out these remaining energies of hope?" finishes the lord of the void and all things of darkness. A dark and gangly figure gazes out upon the skyline of skyscrapers of a downtown city, not taking his glance away from the activity below.

"Well, Master, as you see, our methods of fear, torture, and subjugation have the humans under our spell of organized anarchy, convinced of the illusion of peace," answers Lord Destruction.

"Their species' obsession on the conquest of power, competition of possessions, and miseducation has had them completely misled and uninterested in the truth of humanities," states Lord Chaos.

"Yet and still, the energies of the ancient earth children manage to arise from the ashes of their destruction, like roaches time and time again. Refusing to be a conquered being, the humans' cries of truth are futile. Trials of bonding with the cosmic energies in their attempts to join with a champion obtaining the spirit of no surrender or no retreat, to brave and traverse the storm of debauchery and treachery have been unsuccessful. Any fires of hope have most easily been ousted with the promise of title, authority, and wealth," implies Lord Destruction.

"Our largest complications have been picking up on strong, consistent cosmic life-energy readings of those descendants with potential. Man's emotions and intentions fluctuate so much that it is difficult to identify the humans who are linked to their ancestral knowledge. Like blips on a radar, they come and go. The species' consumed time on meaningless pursuits and defense of self-preservation have dominated the tides for centuries. We can now move into what the humans call the endangered-species stage of the ancient warrior mystics. We have almost completely exterminated or oppressed all the world's warriors of unity and peace. The humans have all but forgotten entirely the ways of their ancestors, blind to the true power of their unity as one. The strength in the division of the human species devastates the balance in between Father Universe and Mother Earth's celestial essence," explains Lord Chaos.

"Even so, having a few centuries passed, and yet a band of humans that have tapped into their acute nature and more than a few of those giftedly sounded creatures began to answer to the calling that's ringing in the pits of their souls. They discovered the untapped energy that manifest in their originality, and to their untrained ears, they understood the tongues of their dead ancestors, seeking out apprentices and followers to vanguard their revolutionary charge," proclaims the gaunt figure peering out beyond the horizon.

"Evident that no matter if we beat them, torture them, or lock them up; the spirits of the earth children are not easily defeated with the means of physicality. Their spirits and energies are not that of a conquered people. If there is one with a connection to the cosmic realm and the spirit to fight, they will forever have a slither of hope. And we must extinguish that hope at all cost!" orders the lord of darkness and the void.

"Fortunately, most of the lesser minions have captured and maintained the essential pillars of the human's institutions of life, the spiritually unfit and unguarded are easily possessed. Most are so feared into position to not even answer the call to be warriors, but fear is not enough. Lord Chaos, Lord Destruction, relay the order to all field generals and their spirit hounds to prepare to go hunting. We must wipe out any possibilities of any rise of a prophetic savior!"

"Yes, Master, with pleasure." The two demonic entities are salivating as they answer the call of their decrepit master.

"Sizzle! Sizzle! Sizzle!" Sounds of a frying pan and the smell of fresh sautéed peppers and onions on a stove being cooked by a high school junior on a Friday evening pervade the room.

"Iesha, the Philly cheese are almost done!" yells Ronin while he works his post at the stove, doing his best impression of his mom in the kitchen. He likes standing in the kitchen taste testing for his mom or looking over her shoulders, keeping a watchful eye on her techniques that he would later practice at his leisure. Ronin has become quite handy with a spatula, and that's because Ronin likes to eat. "I'm pretty sure I will be getting a call from Paul soon to talk about a time for the party. I am actually going to attempt to get in a thirty-minute power nap, he thinks to himself hurry up in the shower!" Ronin shouts to his sister, who's preparing herself in the bathroom. Ronin is now eyeing the stove's digital clock, which reads 7:15 p.m. Next, he tastes a small bit of steak and then dashes a spec of salt and pepper into the frying pan.

"Sittin' up in my room..." Iesha sings along with the tune on her media player, standing and looking at her reflection as she combs through her thick, damp hair. Iesha contemplates on the new group of associates that she will be hanging out with this evening and their fondness about boys. Before today's conversations, her interests in boys are little to nonexistent. Iesha has identified herself as being one of the tomboyish, bookworm types, especially roughhousing and tagging along with her brother. She cannot bring herself to believe that she agrees to be pulled into a night out of her books from a group other than Ronin and Paul. These are the girls that sit around reading magazines and stayed current with the latest BET's top ten hit list; usually Iesha makes fun of the girls entertained by less-intellectual topics. But she is in high school now, sophomore at that, and maybe, it is time to start branching into her own social network in exploring the world. Parting her hair down the middle of her scalp and pulling one side of here curly black hair, she begins to pull her curls into a ponytail, then does the same to the opposite puff of hair. Iesha then self-consciously looks at her chest area and pushes her cleavage, or what little she has, upward to give them a boost, and for a moment, she says, thinking to herself, *If only they were bigger!* She does not want to be flat-chested forever.

Iesha smirks and laughs at herself, pondering on rejecting the whole idea of the party, but Ronin going to the same party makes it even harder to avoid the mixer. She does notice something though—that her associates and probably every person attending the party has what she has not, an identity outside the world of books.

"Iesha, you better make this your best effort to get into some adventure."

Iesha then wraps herself in a bath towel and heads from the upstairs restroom to her bedroom. Entering her bedroom, Iesha makes a beeline toward her closet. She feels apprehensive at the sight of her normal attire—a team jersey or plaid shirt, jeans, and sneakers. Tonight, she wants to be a little daring, walking on this new, adventurous path of hers. Rummaging through her wardrobe, she attempts to piece together an outfit, then she hears a call from downstairs. It's Ronin shouting, letting her know that their Philly cheese subs are almost complete and harping about shower time. "Silly boy, I'm already out of the shower," she mumbles. Iesha then glances at the clock. It reads 7:15 p.m. "I got some time. Paul and EA never get here on time when they give a time." She goes on going about her business of throwing together an outfit constructively using her energies.

Bzzrt! Bzzrt! Bzzrt! A vibrating cell phone and jingle alerts Ronin as he stands inside his kitchen. Chomping down on one of his creations of a Philly cheese subs that he had just prepared for dinner, along with some sweet potato fries, the meal never had a chance of survival. The phone call is just a slight delay in the contents demise.

Bzzrt! Bzzrt! Bzzrt! Ronin is fidgeting around with his dinner plate. In one hand, he's trying to balance it. He almost drops it as he pops his pinky and index fingers into his mouth, one from the other, removing the dripping mayonnaise from the tips of his fingers. He reaches into his pocket to remove his cell phone.

"Homeboy!" Paul Grigg's high-pitched voice comes through the phone's speaker. "What it do? Tell me, you are ready to get it poppin' because tonight is going to be bananas!"

"Ready as I'm ever going to be," replies Ronin, continuing to gobble on his sub and fries. "I just need to jump in the shower and throw on some clothes. I hope to get a quick power nap in too."

"I'm going to act as if I didn't just hear that and not entertain the argument of you taking a power nap at a time like this. But anyway, EA should be through in about an hour to get me. He has to go to some dinner with his parents. Then we will be there to scoop you up," explains Paul.

"I need my power naps!" Ronin pokes and barks at Paul. "Besides, it is plenty enough time for me to power nap and throw on gear, knowing you two anyway. And I'm sure Iesha will be tagging along. She found herself a group of "associates" to mingle with."

"Baby sis is stepping out tonight. She is starting to adjust to the high school vibe. Squad out tonight!" says Paul. "But whatever you gotta do, get it in, bro. We should be there no later than 8:45 p.m. or 9:00 p.m. at the latest."

"We will be ready. Ya'll just be safe riding. Just hit me when ya'll touchdown," responds Ronin.

"All right, later," says Paul.

"Later!"

Click.

Quickly gobbling down the remaining of his sweet potato fries, Ronin throws the edges of brown bread crust into the kitchen's garbage can, then his plate into the dishwasher. He grabs a lime-flavored Gatorade from the fridge and takes a drink; he finishes half the bottle in two big gulps, returning the bottle to the refrigerator. Then Ronin heads out of the kitchen. "Next situation to get into is shower!" Striding up the stairs, Ronin shouts loud as he passes the bedroom door of Iesha. "Iesha, food's ready, and it's on point, as always! I'm jumping in the shower. Paul and EA should be here no later than nine. Be ready!" He hears the muffled response of Iesha from behind her closed door, confirming that she has heard his message.

Ronin steps into his bedroom to grab a pair of boxer shorts, a shirt, and his bath towel. Before he exits the room, he stops at his stereo system and cranks the speakers at full blast, knowing that his mom would be in later that evening. "Party time!" He hips and hops himself into the bathroom.

Squeak! Squeak! Squeak! Hissssss! Ronin starts up the shower, and not wasting time, he removes his dirty wardrobe. He wants to be most efficient with the time he had. "Time to get my equilibrium together," Ronin tells himself, then jumps into the warm and steaming shower.

At the same time, Iesha, in her bedroom, is losing in an epic wrestling match, attempting to fit into a pair of pants that her mom had brought earlier in the year for Christmas. *Bump! Bump!* Iesha slips and loses her footing and rolls onto her bed. Next, she slides, hitting the floor. "Stupid capris! I haven't gained that much weight since Christmas!" she exclaims as she wiggles to squeeze into the pants. Taking one deep breath, she tucks in her tummy. *Ziiip!* "Got it!" she says as she pushes herself upward from the floor. The slender, long-legged, light-brown-complexioned, and bespectacled Iesha stands in front of her body-length mirror, sizing up the fit and feel of her denims. "These look cute, but now if I could just not breathe or have to use the restroom for the next four hours, I would be just fine," says Iesha. Feeling too restricted and short of breath, she begins the challenge of removing the jeans. "All this to hang out! Wow! We will not be making this a regular event!" she utters.

About five minutes of time has passed, Ronin is still soaking in the warm waters, letting the soreness of his body capitalize on the massage by the warm splatters of water droplets. He then rinses the soapsuds from his body after a good lather. Turning off the shower faucet, he gropes for his bath towel proceeding to mop his body dry. Ronin then dresses himself in his undergarments and heads to his bedroom to have his power nap.

*****

The narration of a mystic voice is being carried across the winds: "You are still young, but you have begun to notice and have questioned the dangers of people putting their complete faith and trust in leaders as divinely guided and anointed people, believing they could do no wrong, make no mistakes, or had any human flaws or weaknesses. Time and time again throughout history, the collective species of man has no inclination of true unity and dignity. Anger can blind the vision, and living off the energies of hate and rage, one can be consumed by its own fire, spontaneously combusting. Soon, the sun will descend upon the earth. Absolute unity is the source to the power of liberating the minds, which translates to an unconquerable people. The evil energies of the world manifest to break that unity and the power that grows from it. The light of hope has all but burned out against the tide of those evil energies. Would Father Universe, the creator of all, send another champion to uphold the front lines against the truly evil entities? The reemergence of pride in your true lineage is most vital!"

A kaleidoscope montage rapidly displays optical scenes of human warfare and natural disasters and voices of people screaming in agonizing pain. Suddenly, a flash of light. It's Ronin, sprinting at top speed, damn near out of breath. A thundering crack within the concrete on which he ran crumbles from beneath his feet, splitting into an enormous fissure, engulfing him into an endless plunge.

*****

Bzzrt! Bzzrt! Bzzrt! "It's like that now / you better go and get the hump up…"

"Hello!" Ronin jumps just about halfway through his bedroom ceiling from the OutKast ringtone of his cell phone.

"Sounds like you got enough beauty sleep!" Paul's voice implies. "Get yourself together. We'll be there in about fifteen minutes."

"Yeah!" Ronin's sluggish response ends the call with a click. He lays his head back unto his pillow. Ronin feels the moist spot where his head lay. Drenched in sweat, he feels his undershirt clung to his chest, also soaked in his perspiration; he growls. "So much for the shower before the power nap," he exclaims. Ronin rapidly moves to grab his towel and dashes back to the bathroom. "Iesha, the guys will be here in twenty minutes!"

Currently standing, Iesha is dressed in black spandex leggings, a pair of black-and-white Nike Air Max 95, and a black-and-white Dwayne Wade Miami Heat jersey. "Cute and comfortable!" says Iesha to herself. She brushes her thick, natural shoulder-length hair and uses the reflection in her vanity mirror to braid her hair, twisting her curls into two drooping tails at the sides of her head.

"Dare to be different," says Iesha, then pulls open a drawer to her makeup box, taking a stick of lip gloss and lines the contour of her lips. "Mama always said I could be pretty, if I would stop trying to run behind Ronin all the time," she mutters. Satisfied with the look of her attire, Iesha switches off her bedroom light with a click and heads out of her room.

Hustling to get through his second shower, Ronin rushes to his room, knowing that Paul and EA will be outside at any moment; the last thing he wants is to hear Paul talking smack about him not being ready because of his power nap. He dives into his closet snatching a pair of long blue denims that had a tan wash and jumps inside. Ronin throws on a pair of crew socks, then stuffs his feet into a pair of Nike Dunk SB Low Pro Jedi. Simultaneously, a car honks.

"A-yo, bro! We out here!" Ronin hears the horn and calling of Paul from outside. Not giving too much attention to his fashion, Ronin grabs a T-shirt from one of his closet shelves and sprays himself with a mist of cologne. Gathering his cell phone and house keys, Ronin leaves his room.

"Well, damn, look at you!" exclaims Ronin with a look of surprise on his face. "Is this my kid sister that I'm looking at?" He's impressed with the fashion taste of Iesha. "Do I need to pull out the guns?" Laughs Ronin, amused, and they both chuckle inside their foyer.

"No need to get all big brother on me. I just decided to try a new look. Be different," says Iesha, attempting to keep Ronin's protective nature at ease.

"All right, I'm just saying. I don't want to have to get into it with anybody about my sister," replies Ronin.

"Trust me, I know," states Iesha. "Did you already let Ma know that we are leaving?" she asks.

"Yeah, I sent her a text earlier when I was cooking. I let her know that we were heading out for a few hours with the fellas tonight. You know she does not mind if we make it back by 12:30 a.m. She said that she should be getting in not too long from now," explains Ronin.

"Cool, got your keys?" asks Iesha.

"Yeah, got 'em." Ronin flashes his key ring, confirming.

"Don't forget to keep the lights on!" reminds Iesha, and out the door they go.

They step out into the night. The weather is not too humid; there is not a cloud to be seen, and the moon illuminates the sky with its lucid, pale glow.

"What's up, my people? What it do?" addresses Paul, sticking his head out of the passenger side of EA's SUV. Music is pumping in the back. "Ya'll ready to roll?" asks Paul.

"What's up, PG?" salutes Ronin.

"Hey, guys!" greets Iesha.

"Looks like somebody has caught on the high school wave already," states Paul, referring to Iesha as they set foot into the back seat of the mini SUV. Wearing a contoured look and glance—that suggested to not press the issue from Ronin. EA turns up the radio's volume, switches gears, and accelerates into the dark.

Riding out to the tunes of EA's playlist and listening to the pair of mates wildly telling stories of their time at the mall as well as after-school events, and even gossiping on those attending tonight's event, Ronin cannot help but drift off in his mind, mulling over the strange dreams and visions that he has been having. "Hey, Iesha," he says in subtle tune.

"What's up, Ron?" inquires Iesha.

"Have you ever had a dream and—" he asks, with a prolonged pause as if he could not find the words.

"What is it?" Iesha nudges.

"It's just these dreams that I have been having lately. It's like I keep hearing voices, seeing crazy visions, and I keep waking up in these cold sweats," Ronin explains to his sister.

"Sounds more like nightmares to me, but you have always been one to put a lot of thought into things. You are pretty hard on yourself," responds Iesha. "The only time I ever feel my anxiety attacking me like that are around test-taking periods. Maybe it's just something that has been bugging you about the game this week?" Iesha suggests, trying to reassure her brother to not make too much fuss about his visions.

"Yeah, maybe you're right. I have been trying to put it out of my mind. Hopefully tonight out with baby sister and her new swag may help the case," responds Ronin. Iesha and Ronin both burst out in laughter; then they return to the jovial conversation of friends Paul and EA.

"Oh, I should text the girls and let them know that we will be out there shortly," adds Iesha.

About twenty-five minutes later, south bound on Florida's Interstate 95, they head west off the City of Basin Worth's exit ramps. EA, being a Basin Worth native, easily bobs and weaves through the back roads, making short work of Friday's night traffic. Not even half a block from the address of the party's location, the guys just about lost their minds with excitement from the line of vehicles positioned along the narrow street curbs.

"Man, there's nowhere to park. It's like the president died or something!" shouts Paul halfway out of the SUV as the creep up the street fishing for a parking spot.

And as if a lightning bolt had hit him, EA jumps up in his seat. "Eureka! I know. We can park at Mr. Buckley's. He lives right up the street. I've been cutting his grass for years. He and my old man go way back. We can just pull up there, and if he comes out, it won't be a problem. He'll know it's my truck," he says.

"EA, my brother from another mother, white people power. That's major!" expresses Paul.

"For real, dope!" adds Ronin.

Immediately after parking and exiting from EA's truck, the group can hear the sounds of the loud music booming throughout the block. The disc jockey is shouting names and hyping up the crowd. The group's adrenaline all runs high in anticipation.

"Yo, tonight is going to be epic!" says Paul.

"I'm right there with you on that!" concurs EA. The two boys are speaking on the night as a legendary tale of adventure in high school party-going. And at this point, it is even hard for Ronin not to be showing signs of jitters from the excitement.

Resembling a scene out of a motion picture, the atmosphere is electric. The number of the crowd has to be well over three hundred, at minimum. It is a melting pot of complexion, both male and female. There's a variety of ages and different groups representing various schools and local cities that make up Providencia County. With girls dressed in seminude attire, revealing flesh fill the streets. Their hips draw the eyes of the sharp and slicked-tongue males, whose mouths flirted with lust of the body on his mind, sending the boys into a state of euphoria. The sight is quite unbelievable. The smell of Caribbean cooking and barbecue leads the group to its first stop among the crowd.

"Shouts out to my boy Byron!" the DJ says over the speakers. "Celebrating my dawg's birthday, got the block shut down! We out here for you, my boy!" and then he cuts back into mixing the track, the concrete vibrating from the amplification of the speakers. Entranced by the melody, the gang staggers backward and forward, stepping and bopping with other attendees standing and waiting in line at the Caribbean street vendor's stand.

"Beef patties and coco bread never smelled so good! I hate to admit it, but I'm not thinking about the game right now!" bursts out Ronin, grinning with joy.

"I told you, man. You had to be here!" yells Paul.

Not containing her excitement any better from the experience of being in the presence of jubilant energy, Iesha's heart is just about to jump through her chest. Just as the guys' hormones are jumping wild, Iesha's womanhood is going bonkers too with ecstasy from the various styles of baggy pants and flashy gold chains and teeth. Captivated by the groove of the music, she lets her body sway and rock. Not being under the watchful eye of her mom, she can be a bit loose. Ronin's mind is preoccupied with the crowd; Iesha is anxiously ready to find her group of associates. She is not looking to put anything else into her stomach, so she leaves the beef patties and coco bread to the guys.

"So what's up, Iesha? Think you can hang with the big dawgs?" pokes Paul. "Where ya girls at?"

"Oh please! Haven't been left behind yet, and let the letter tell it, I am actually ahead!" she shoots back. She and Paul are always making it good at sparring jokes. "But I am not sure where they are.

I told them that I am out here." Her eyes scan across the number of attendees in the crowd. The boys are currently munching on coco bread and beef patties, quenching their appetite.

Ding! Iesha gets a hit in her text message inbox: "Where are you? We are by the DJ's booth!"

After surveying the horde of partygoers and mapping the best route toward the DJ's booth, Ronin and his teammates convoy Iesha through the maze of people, wading through the waves of faces, nodding, waving, and embracing with former classmates and teammates as well. A person who would be hard to miss, towering over any crowd, teammate Big Dee is spotted. Big Dee lives not too far from Ronin and Paul in another apartment complex and has carpooled with teammates Mike and Matt. Identified, they join the pack as they get within eye distance of the DJ's booth. Not wanting to postpone her rendezvous any longer, Iesha breaks from the group of teammates to go ahead while they huddle in humorous chatter.

"Ron, I'm going to go ahead to the booth to get with the girls!" she shouts to Ronin.

"Okay. Hey, do you have your phone?" he asks.

"Yes, right here!" She flashes her phone and safely tucks it inside her female storage place. "It's on vibrate, and the ringer is on full blast!"

"All right, man, you be careful," he says, and they embrace.

"I will," says Iesha, then she continues parting the crowd, disappearing among the mass.

To Ronin, hanging out with the guys on the weekends always feels like being in a bunch of young deer or elk during the season of rut, with Paul and Big Dee leading the way in most of the rutting. But Ronin will not exchange the group of buddies he has for the world, no matter how off-the-wall they could be. Even though they are at a party, it feels as if they were chilling and hanging in their own universe; one cannot notice that they had just lost in their playoff game the previous night. At that present time, none of that matters.

"Byron got the block lit!" says Big Dee. "Them boys got that cake!"

"You know he fucks with Tony, and he is plugged in with his cousin Duke," states Paul "He's the man of the city!"

Acts of defiance and terror have turned men like Duke into anti-heroes or parasites to their community, depending on one's outlook. Duke and countless other men have mastered the art of smiling at people in their faces while exploiting those who have never learned to think, extracting money from them. They soon become lofty and arrogant with their larger incomes; their hearts and souls show no bond with those they have forgotten, with no escape from the slums of the ghetto.

Both Paul and Big Dee, at center stage, keep the attentions of their teammates entertained with gossip of the neighborhood hierarchy. Elsewhere in the crowd, like a sponge, Iesha stands there observing the scene of her associates—glistening sweat and gyrating their bodies to the music while laughing and shunning off the attention of the boys encircled around them observing and throwing themselves to participate. Thinking of never having the nerve to be center stage doing anything besides a book-report presentation, Iesha tries to play it cool as she watches.

"Girl, these niggas out here are so thirsty!" bellows Kenia, as the three girls take a break from dancing to catch their breaths.

"Yeah, you can always tell the ones that don't really have any money!" spats Tammy.

"For real!" encourages Kenia on the comment.

"You don't dance?" Sheena asked Iesha.

"I do, just not in front of people," answers Iesha, her face dressed in an awkward demeanor.

The girls can sense from the embarrassed glance on Iesha's face her lack of experience in being out in front of the crowd.

"I'm not much of a people person," says Iesha.

"Stop being green. You just gotta loosen up and get out more!" says Kenia.

"Can't be all books and no play. It's all good though. We got you. We are used to the fast life," insists Tammy.

"Where is your brother? Didn't you come out here with him?" asks Sheena.

"Yes, I did. He is out here somewhere with his teammates," replies Iesha, receptive of the comments and unique points of views that she is being exposed to.

*****

"I'm telling you, bro. I wanted to hit this nigga on the bus, bro! Tryin' me in front of my niggas, acting like super save a nigga and shyt! He's lucky I didn't have my tool on me!" an agitated younger brother informs to his older brother, tailgating among their band of six.

"Just glad your trigger-happy ass didn't have it. Li'l bro, you bring too much heat to yourself, and you pick the wrong time and place to bring it," says the elder. "Least, you got to the pickup on time, and I didn't have to once again get Duke off your ass. No telling how much shyt we would be in if you missed that drop this morning. You gotta chill out, especially until we get done with the work. Keep calm. Cousin or not, Duke will get our ass both missing. But fuck all that, did you finish counting the money?"

"Yeah, it's all there," answers the younger brother, tossing a stack of one-hundred-dollar bills wrapped with rubber bands into a bag filled with additional bundles of twenty-, ten-, and five-dollar bills.

"Now we just wait for Duke to pull up. Where the beans at?" asks the elder.

The younger brother, still vexed about the scrutiny of his manhood, heeds the warning from his older brother and puts his focus aside from the vengeful thoughts. He then digs out of his pocket a small tied sandwich bag. Inside it are these candy-like objects; they resemble Skittles or M&Ms, in all sorts of colors—red, blue, green. But one can tell from the packaging that this candy item is not found at your ordinary convenience or grocery store. The brothers each take one of the candy objects and tosses them into their mouths, ingesting the items.

"Double up!" says the elder and takes another, following it with a drink from a water bottle. The younger brother serves the remaining members of the group as if serving up cheese and wine at a mixer.

*****

After about an hour and a half of jovial laughter and dancing, the crowd is in a prime mood for the party. There is a hazy mist that has fallen across the night's sky as time approaches closer to the midnight hour. The DJ continuously woofs up the crowd and shouts out names and announcements, pumping energy and momentum. The females are sweating and moving their bodies; the male's prurient urges are raging from the pheromones released by their mates. Eyes are being widened, and cultures are being shocked. The way the night is going seems to be too good to be true, but soon, our young faithful will learn that everything that glitters is not gold and there is always that one petulant spirit that spoils it for the bunch.

Stalking the streets' crowd of festive people, a leader and his gang, like a pack of starving hyenas, are participating in a duel between the hunter and the hunted. Perfectly in tune with their hunting environment, yet every situation brings an unexpected challenge. The predators calculate which of its many strategies to use to catch its prey, and rightfully so, because in this contest, even for the most skilled, success is not a guarantee. The pack's alpha leads the way in their efforts to work as a team scouting for prospects; it does not take long in their prowling before they spot what they are looking for. With a sinister smile, the leader takes his approach, catching his prey's attention off guard with a quick pounce from behind.

"Well, damn, fresh meat. Two times in one day. I'm starting to think this is not a coincidence. I think you just might be meant for me!"

Spinning around, Iesha is caught off guard from the unexpected greetings of an unidentified presence. Iesha's eyes turn as wide as grapefruits, and her tonsils are halfway up her throat, as she attempts to gather her composure. "The guy from school!" she utters.

The smiling, gold-teeth-wearing upperclassman is sporting jeans, a pair of Air Jordan's, T-shirt, and gold chain. "Let me find out if you like to go bump in the night!" he shoots his line.

Iesha, a bit taken back from the upperclassman's aggressive and seasoned approach, is at a loss for words, not having much to say. She throws a smirk instead, not knowing how to respond, contemplating to herself, *Where in the hell is Ronin right now?* wishing for the blanket of her brother's protection. *What am I going to say? I don't have class right now to use as an excuse.* "There isn't much to find out!" she sasses back, making her response short and direct. Something about Iesha's cagey behavior has excited the upperclassman in the pursuit of his hunt.

"Well, damn. Don't be like that. You mean to tell me I can't get any of your time?"

Iesha can tell from the persistent nature and the arrogance of his speech that this guy is not used to hearing the word *no*, or he does not take too kindly to rejection. And for some reason, he has his eyes set on her. "I don't have that much time to spare," she smartly comments, hoping that her blunt response will give a clue to the unwanted attention, but it is futile.

"But you're out here. Come on, don't be so mean!" he returns in his attempts to catapult his opposition's defenses.

"God, send me a miracle," she whispers in a puff. Instantly with those words, Iesha hears the high-pitched voice of her new associate Kenia. "Hey, Tony!"

Swiftly stepping in, Kenia, Tammy, and Sheena, take position in front of Iesha, something like the act of a herd of courageous African buffalo guarding a lost calf that strayed too far away from the flock, their horns displayed at full tilt. The predator, now thrown off himself from the miscalculation of his strategy, realizes he made a mistake. Quickly he maneuvers to mask his guard against the shift in momentum. "Tammy, Sheena, and Kenia—the last three I expected to see you with, fresh meat!" Staring into the gauging faces of Kenia and Sheena, Tony finds himself in a stalemate.

"I can only imagine what you had in mind," says Tammy in a cold tone.

Not able to keep eye contact with Tammy as she shoots her gaze of hate at Tony. "I'm just chillin', tryin' to introduce myself to a new face."

Iesha can sense that obviously there is some sort of history between the two parties from the hostility in Tammy. "I'd be damned she'd want anything from what you had to offer!" snaps Tammy. Sheena and Kenia both snicker at the comment. Failing to get the expected results in his ambush attempt, Tony decides to cut his losses and looks to make an escape from the morass he found himself. He becomes a bit at ease when his pack members, minus one, has caught up to him taking the sight of conversation as an invitation to join the affair. Tony is completely thrown off by the companionship of the girls and clearly unprepared to expend the energy going further into a debate with an audience. "No need to get hot 'bout ya friend, li'l mama, just checking out the scenery. But do ya thang. We got money to get to anyway!" And with the snap of his finger, he leads his pack scurrying off throughout the crowd. Immediately, a distressed message of "WHERE ARE YOU?!!" is sent out by Iesha to her brother, Ronin.

*****

Deeply engaged in the amusement of people watching and cracking jokes about one another, Ronin and his team of friends makes the most of their time-out with one another. No mentions of last night's loss in the playoffs, no worries about classmates making ignorant comments, just good fun hanging out. Currently, the boys are having a debate about the best burger in the city, "You're not from Providencia Beach County if you've never had a burger from Hamburger Heaven," expresses Big Dee. "Best burgers and chili dogs in the county, hands down!"

"But what about Five Guys?" questions Matt.

"Like I said, Slim Shady, you're not from Providencia Beach if you've never eaten at Hamburger Heaven. Five Guys is decent, but I need more than big and greasy for my ten dollars!"

"For real!" both Ronin and Paul agree to the statement. The guys on the team knew that Matt is new to Providencia Beach, having just moved their last season.

"Don't worry, bro. We will get you downtown to check it out," says Paul.

The entire night the crowd has a nonstop flow to its traffic. People were shifting and flowing along the block, unintentionally bumping in passing, expressing, "excuse mes" and "my bads." So not giving much attention to a bump from behind, Ronin turns to pardon himself for being in the passer's pathway. He and the passer turn to regard each other. Locking eyes, they instantly recognize the familiar faces of each other. Ronin knows he is the young alpha whom he had got into an altercation with earlier that morning on the bus. A blazing stare of hate burns from the young alpha's gaze; Ronin can feel the smoldering orbs setting fire to his skin.

"The nigga from this morning!" the young alpha screams, and without warning, he lunges upward into a swing, his fist clenched and aimed toward Ronin's face. Not having more than a split second, Ronin catches a glimpse of the punch coming. Pumped with more than enough exhilaration and anticipation, Ronin dips down and ducks under the wailing fists. The group of boys and near-standing crowd are totally caught off guard by combative scene. Ronin, a bit surprised by his opponent's actions, calmly sidesteps and backs away from wildly thrown punches. The young alpha locks in, his nose desiring to be filled with the smell of the blood of his enemy, his mind absent of anything but vengeance. Throwing caution to the wind about anything or anyone around him, the young alpha lunges ferociously at Ronin, not paying attention to the towering six foot and eight inch, 240-pound teammate, and friend of Ronin creeping from his rear. Big Dee with a quick two-step motion closes the distance between him and the assailant, grabbing both arms of the young alpha, restraining him into a full Nelson position.

"Chill out, li'l bro! Chill out!" yells Big Dee, easily manhandling the young alpha like a ragdoll. Now fully subdued and being hit further with humiliation, the young alpha grows even wilder at the prevention of revenge.

By now, a little over half of the parties' attention has turned to the scuffle. Cutting into his mix to keep the crowd controlled, the DJ says, "We out here having a good time for my dawg's birthday. We don't need to start acting wild! We ain't tryin' to have 'trol shut us down!" Then he cuts back into his mix, but this time, instead of continuing his fast mix, he cuts into a much slower record to ease the crowd.

"You good?" screams Big Dee at the young man, restrained in his arms, not giving any means of movement.

"I'm cool!" yells the young man, giving in because he knows he is at a loss, releasing himself from the grip.

"Ron, you cool?" asks Big Dee.

"Cooler than a polar bear's toenail!" responses Ronin, using one of his favorite lines from an OutKast record.

Big Dee gives way to the Nelson hold on the young alpha, keeping him at bay and a watchful eye on the attacker as he drops his arms and gathers himself. The young alpha spins to get a look at his restraint, and he sees the towering mass, stares him in the face, and shoots him a death beam of hate.

"All right," the young alpha says in a tone of surrender, grasping a good look at Ronin and his collective, "all right!" then he walks away.

The eyes of the crowd follow him as he wanders into the gloom of the horizon. Ronin, acting nonchalantly, is instantly bombarded with questions about the who, what, and why of the situation from his crew.

"Yo! What the fuck?" exclaims Paul.

"How in the hell did that just happen? Bro, do you know who that was?"

The noise of chatter floats throughout the crowd.

"Bro, take a breath," says Ronin. "He was just some jit that I got into it with on the bus this morning. I stopped him from making fun of some old man, nothing serious."

"Bro, you just got into with one of the hottest li'l niggas in the city! That was Tony's little brother, Mike-Mike. That's hella serious to beef with them boys. My boy, you tough, but them niggas plugged in, and they got guns and shyt!" explains Big Dee.

Ronin understands most of the workings of the street code. His friends' warnings are not to be taken lightly; he will need to be on his toes and not give any chance of taking his enemy for granted. He reaches into his pocket, taking out his cell phone to read the message from his sister, Iesha: "WHERE ARE YOU?!!"

*****

85

Crouched in a sitting position behind a parked car just up the street of the party, Mike-Mike—the young alpha male, absent in mind of all thoughts of logic and reason—vows to get his revenge in some way from his humiliation; blood is on his mind.

"This fuck nigga, think he want it. Fuck him and his people. Anybody can get it, pussy-ass nigga!" he says in soliloquy. From under the car's passenger back wheel, he pulls a small chrome firearm—a .380 semi-automatic handgun. He cocks the pistol's chamber, then heads back in the direction of the party. Standing at the edge of the crowd, Mike-Mike scans the crowd, searching for his enemies. He spots them bunched in the middle of the crowd. He thinks it stupid to go into the crowd, so he walks a few paces to a secluded area, stretches out his arm to the sky, and he pulls the trigger. Three shots in the air. *Pop! Pow! Pow!* sends the crowd into a swelling stampede. Partygoers scatter in various directions, frantic and oblivious of the source of the gunfire. Amid chaos, Mike-Mike manages to lock eyes again with Ronin from yards away, and he takes aim.

CHAPTER 6

EARTH CHILDREN HAD WALKED THE surface of the planet for 1,818,036 years. Men and women who had once lived in peace and unity as brothers and sisters of the earth had now grown to perfect their techniques of penetration and dominance, fixing the applied pressures of institutions. The old way of keeping and tending to the secrets and ways of Father Universe and Mother Earth and communicating between the spirit world and human world were no longer the most important. Men took the spirit of Mother Earth and commanded it and controlled it.

Culture and civilization spread. Political power had become predicated on the worth of gold and raw material. Man was completely brainwashed and assimilated; they had been persecuted and tortured into an unimaginative, mediocre, and fearful state. Kings had strengthened their political and economic influence over tribes and clans. They began to believe that they truly could outmaneuver anything, foolishly thinking that stone works would last an eternity. Invincible and powerful in their vanity, they believed they could outmaneuver death.

But the fall of the true spirit of the earth children did not mean that the earth children surrendered. For thousands of years, men of goodwill and true humanitarian spirit in the mother country had been dying with courage and dignity for the cause of harmony and balance. Tribes and clans would liberate their territories for a short time—maybe a few days or a few months or a few years at the most. But eventually through means of espionage and military power, the oppressors would wipe out their gains. Having neither the strength nor the organization, the clans and tribes were powerless. Man's religion had become the guise to the real aims of wealth, power, and world domination by the men who saw god in themselves; evil men drive to conquer and enslave the mind thus vitiating man's spirit. For a proud and dignified spirit, fighting was the only way to resist subjugation and dehumanization, having their deep concern about the future generations, and the welfare of the preservation of their way of life. The earth children, filled with the spirit, knew that if they submitted to the will of man's religion and exploitation, they would destroy their cosmic bond and condemn them to a living death. Furthermore, it would be a great injustice to their posterity to lose the stories and achievements of their ancestors.

The resisting earth children kept to their old ways of not using a written language. They possessed a complex and rich oral tradition, passing history from generation to generation in spoken form. Writing had become a symbol of representing self in glorification of those who had learned to inscribe. For the ones that stood with pride in the true spirit of humanity, it came with grave cost. Not converting to the religion of the time would bring warfare, resulting in complete execution, enslavement, or being driven from the land. Millions chose death over slavery and persecution. Women loyal to their men would follow their men to hell; many of the women would attack armed men fiercely seeking death, following the leads of the brave men in warrior spirit. Men and women could not bear the loss of their self-identity being torn away from their roots with their past, losing the very links with their heritage and the essentials of the universe from which they got their meaning of strength and inspiration.

Self-preservation and self-interests had led many earth children to become brutal to their own kind, knowing what they were doing in pursuit of weapons, power, and riches. Weapons are given strategically to certain tribes and clans seeking to become big and wealthy powers, expanding their territories over the smaller tribes. This built animosity would set forward a path of never-ending tribal and clan warfare among the humans, creating an everlasting hatred between groups, destroying the basis for unity.

A massive entity of dark energy laughed in amusement at his epic plot. "Ha ha, pathetic humans! Gold, weapons, and warfare would keep them so hating and tirelessly fighting each other that they would never know who their real enemy was! The scheme was to make humans separate themselves in groups—the veil of ethnic superiority because of blood. Giving privileges and opportunities to one that will be denied by the other creates mutual hatred that will make unity impossible. It is most significant to remember that up until this time, since prehistory, there was no titles of Negro referring to dark earth children, nor any titles of Caucasian to refer to the lighter earth children. Not all earth children had kept their jet-black or dark complexions. Countless centuries of living and adapting to cool climates resulted in lighter pigmentation. This simple yet pivotal factor to the existence of the human species will soon be forgotten, and their energies consumed in division and war, limiting their cognitive potential to a feeble state."

Scattered across the lands, thousands of earth children's daily agenda was of survival—nothing more, nothing less—going months of the year with nothing more to feed the children with than tree bark and dirt. Periods when discoveries of meals, which may last two or three weeks, caused for celebration, but later findings that all the streams, rivers, and watering holes have all but dried up. Babies clinging to their mother's with skeleton-like body frames, their bellies protruding from hunger, were carried off to the shade of a bush or tree to die. There were various results for different tribes. Some perished. Some became nomads. Many tribes and clans merged with other lost and separated families, developing different languages and cultures, thriving only in some of the most inhabitable and desolate areas of the mother country.

Before 3000 BC, much of the Sahara was green and fertile. Its inhabitants were hunters at first and then, in time, cattle herders; their societies were stable and had developed. But the collective ravaging of Mother Earth's substance, eventually caused dramatic change in climate, destroyed the fertile pastureland, and the Sahara expanded. Structured like a massive plateau, there were no paths to the interior from the ocean. The Nile River and its six cataracts were the only accessibly navigated routes from the Atlantic. Now they had become the center crossroads in all directions leading to Africa, Asia, and Europe.

For 3,300 years before the Christian era, Egypt was split into two kingdoms: Upper and Lower Egypt. King Menes was the first pharaoh to establish the Egyptian dynasty and to unite what was known as the Two Lands by conquest from Asian invaders. Before this period, there was no Egypt. it was referred to as Nowe, and for a time, Memphis. Menes established powerful governments and built empires that extended in all directions. From 3100 to 2345 BC, the first five dynasty lineages ruled after unification—the Upper lands representing the hawk and the Lower lands representing the snake. Egypt became the center of power to those of the mother lands. The land of Ethiopia was the nucleus of Mother Earth's life source and the highest concentrated area of her life essence. Egypt became the main object for destruction by non-Ethiopian powers.

Heard were only a few tales of the martyrs and heroes, who fought without surrender or retreat, from works written or studied from often indoctrinated histories of oppressors of true humanity, praising the conqueror and interpreting the humanitarian as criminal or terroristic and often missed the significance between the links that ties the complexities of the social situations at hand in both past and present and how they remain in effect. This collective knowledge passed on from generation to generation embellishes another panorama expressing how the human species had come to its present disposition of power at the expense of his fellow man, links that touch us all as human species. The power and determination of those who fought up against the transplant of the mind did not deny their true heritage by taking the easy way out; instead, gave up the opportunity to direct power, fame, and fortune within man's new society. For as long as there is a small glimpse of hope that exists in man's spirit in a world obsessed with greed, vanity, and self-preservation, there will remain some chance for the true spirit of the earth children and light for a more humane world.

For over five thousand years, the descendants of earth children—ancestors with true humanitarian spirit, hungry and weakened by disease—resisted the domination by the other brother earth nations. Beginning with the time of his brother invaders raiding the mother continent from Asia and then later Europe, they infiltrated from within by process of centuries of amalgamation, taking the secrets and knowledge of tribes, creating battlefronts, flanking one another, depopulating nations with help of various chiefs, kings, and internal figures, seeking wealth and security.

With new power came new influences, and with new influences came new power. Whether it be under the guise of religion, imperialism, colonization, or industrialism, Lord Darkness's stratagem had succeeded and swept across Mother Earth's surface, enthralling Father Universe's prized creations in incessant bloodshed. The acts of the dark entity had infuriated Father Universe; he could not fathom the impetus of his dark counterpart evincing its naive and self-absorbed nature. To brood over his interests in matters of the dark and to contemplate that he could be forgotten, he had lost sight that everything in existence of the cosmic energies were all connected, and all energies had their locus within creation. Even more confounding was that his earth children collectively had forgotten them and allowed themselves to be ensnared in a contest of limited visions of material prosperity, power, and tribal antagonism as the pinnacles of life. Humans ravaged and depleted Mother Earth of her resources.

"The collective human world had been taken over, exploited for wealth, and its people dehumanized and bred through enslavement. Their own energies were manifesting chaos," Father Universe said in consultation with his consort.

Mother Earth, pleading only as the essence of nurturing could for the children who came from the sands of her bosom, said, "My husband, my love, your energies are the beginning and the end that flows through all. They are which that keep us all connected. Do not be so frustrated that the humans have allowed themselves to turn away from us. The dark entity is most cunning. But not all have denied the path of nature, and with those wails from our calling children's energies, the tides of their brothers self-destruction will be turned."

Father Universe was intently absorbing the council of his consort, Mother Earth knowing the empirical allocation with disturbing accuracy. "The thing about it is that I am not upset, just amazed at the ungratefulness. Perhaps that is the problem. I have cosseted the species and given them will of freedom prematurely. Given already are the things needed to be in complete harmony with the balance of the cosmic energies. But man, boastful in his vanity of innovation, self-glory, and self-indulgence, rather deny and destroy the very thing that keeps things alive," said Father Universe.

Father Universe, even though displeased with the ways of his earth children, knew they were a young species up against various mysteries of the universe. They were like a defiant teenager not making the best decisions, half-heartedly completing assignments, skipping out on responsibilities—a real pain in the ass 364 days out of the year. But the hope and faith that presided within, Father Universe believed that on that 365th day, his children would remember Him and have his or her hands enthusiastically raised and assignments completed and chores done. He would be the first there, arms wide, hooting and hollering congratulations at the prodigal child's return. Man's path in life was his to choose, Father Universe constrained himself from directly interfering on earthly affairs, allowing their wills to determine their fate. "If the species of man cannot live in harmony, it is incapable of survival. Men will no longer be judged by his quality as a human individual. Their cries will all be absurdly the same. Maybe there will be some change in detail, but no matter the group, being subjugated, persecuted, or dehumanized will nonetheless result in the same conclusion—them failing to rise above their circumstances. Our children have much to make up as the revolution of their minds and spirits will be a perilous trek up the mountain."

The empires and tribes of Ethiopia had learned of their brother and sister nations of Asia and Europe. Since prehistory and the time of the Asian nations' successful invasion of the Nile Delta in the Lower lands, all the Ethiopian societies saw that their brother nations were relentless to conquer and master the lands of Mother Ethiopia. This resulted in the tribes forming a boundary line between the two lands, which the clans with light complexion were not allowed to settle. Menes' tremendous victory over the Asian nations, unifying the Upper and Lower lands gave birth to what the world knows today as Egypt (before this, it was known as Memphis). Few clans with light complexion were allowed in the Upper lands; Menes attempted to encourage the union of the two kingdoms and the spirit of brotherhood through unification.

It was a bittersweet symphony that this period marked the golden age of the Ethiopian nations that were of dark complexion. They started the dynastic lineage system, established centralized government, and expanded their foreign trade. The first five dynasties held firm power across a span of 750 years under the rule of great leaders, such as Menes, Athothes, Imhotep, Queen Hatshepsut, Queen Candace, and many others. Despite their accomplishments, the policy applied in the spirit of brotherhood would mark the beginning of the eventual downfall of all earth nations and kin of dark pigmentation. There was an extended period designated by a line of a substantial leader, but at the end of the sixth dynasty, weak leaders followed with long reigns of internal disorganization and external chaos; consequently, crushing the centralized government that Menes had established in the first dynasty.

In 2181 BC, on the boundaries of one of the most arcane areas in Ethiopia, the Sudd swamplands; no one in their sane mind would think that any chance of survival could be possible for man here, beyond food for the man-eating crocodiles, swarming mosquitoes, and other stalking creatures. This humid freshwater habitat that stretched as large as England was neither all water nor land. It was an endless scene of clustered islands intertwined with tree vines and branches. The natural phenomenon would serve as a sanctuary from the outside world to one of Mother Earth's remaining practicing tribes of Ethiopia.

Persecuted and forced out from their original lands and homes for not converting from their commitment and duties of the old ways, scattered survivors and nomads from the last remaining tribes of earth spirit merged with one another. Some of the most ancient rituals and skilled warriors lost in the flames of societies were left behind in the fiercest wars between man. The watery swampland acted as a mysterious labyrinth of tall grass to those who had no knowledge of the telepathic bond with the things of nature. In these swamps, one of the last remaining earth children clans fleeing war for survival would find refuge.

*****

Perched high on a tree branch, a water eagle casts its eyes below, stalking the storks and egrets fishing in the marsh. The croaks of the bullfrog below and the creaks and buzzing orchestrated by insects fill the airways. The water eagle watches with anticipation for a moment when one of the young mothering birds gets careless and distracted on one of their plunges. *Plops*—that is the sound of a downed head of an egret, and up comes its crown, quivering as it wrestles with its catch.

Suddenly, the overture of nature's chorus is disturbed by the discussion of two young boys wadding knee-deep through the swamp. The larger boy is tugging at the bow of a canoe while the smaller boy steers its stern. Inside the canoe lay two spears and this twine-like material. They trudge the waterways as their ancestors had in the past century on numerous hunting expeditions.

"Little brother," says the bigger, tall, and muscular boy, "has your spirit animal revealed itself to you yet?" his eyes forward, keeping his head on a swivel.

"No, I have yet to have a vision," answers the smaller boy, not as tall and muscular as his older brother, but still respectfully fit in his stature as well.

"How about you? Have the ancestors come to visit and speak with you in your dreams, brother?" he shoots back to his older brother.

"I have yet to have a vision as well, my brother, but I imagine that my vision would be that of the mighty lion or the powerful gorilla, exactly like our father or his father. Do you see these arms, huh? Look at them!" he eggs on his younger brother. "These arms are made to be mighty and crush mountains by the bloodline of the ancestors!" he shouts. "Come on, tell me what animal spirit it is that you wish to see?"

The younger brother is always amused by the debate he is pulled into by his older brother's points of views. "If I could seek a vision, it would be that of the honey badger or the leopard," he excitedly responds without haste.

"The honey badger or the leopard," repeats the older brother. "Bwahaha! The honey badger or the leopard? Come on, baby brother, out of all the mighty creatures, you choose the honey badger or the leopard? Bwahaha, we may need to send you to one of the other clans!" he joyously taunts his younger brother.

"Oh, shut up! What is wrong with the honey badger or leopard? I like them," exclaims the younger brother, taking his stand, reminiscing over the tales told of the relentless honey badger or the versatile leopard.

"One of these days, you are going to grow out of Grandmother's night tales from when you were a baby at five and understand what true power amounts to," says the older brother.

"Well, you haven't received your vision yet either, so I don't think you have grasped a complete understanding either!" protests the younger brother.

"You will see, just watch for it. My power and strength will bring the biggest catch to the ceremony of names in honor of our baby sister!" declares the older brother.

"Yeah, yeah, you show me!" utters the younger brother as they tussle in their endless feud of words.

*****

"My name is Kamau. This is my older brother, Baaku, and we are the sons of Chief Tua, warrior-king of one of the last surviving tribes of the earth kingdoms. Our grandmother, the tribe's storyteller and former chief, and our great grand father had fled from massacre to this area of water and tall grass as a child with other fragmented earth tribes. Waning in numbers, there were only about one hundred surviving known members of the tribe who made it to the Sudd. There were even fewer members of the tribe who were experienced in the old ways of the cosmic bond and the path of the warrior-mystic, and this includes our grandmother, who was reared by her grandfather. The remaining elders of the tribes had discussed that it was best, as means of survival, to split into four smaller clans to preserve the oral traditions and keep the ancient rituals safe and secret. Annually meeting in ceremonies and social gatherings in honor of the cosmic bond, this is where Grandmother met Grandfather fifty years ago. Our clans of warrior-mystics have thrived here in the swamps the past century, secluded from the outside world, protecting the old ways. And tonight is the naming ceremony in honor of our baby sister.

"The four tribes will gather from their undisclosed locations, remotely scattered throughout the Sudd's boundaries. They will come in celebration, bestowing gifts and presents. Friends and kinsmen will be in joys of laughter, visiting old faces. The elder councils will lead us in the ritual ceremony. The tribes have traditionally bestowed the responsibility of naming a child to the tribe elders, being that the elders are the most skilled at reading the nature of one's spirit energy. They avoid naming a child until he or she is at least four to twelve days of age. Typically, the stronger the cosmic energies bonded with one's nature, the earlier a child would receive its name. I received my name at five days. Baaku got his title at day 7. He always jokes this is because he played with too many boulders. This is a great time because our baby sister has a strong spirit energy. She would be granted her name before any of us at four days."

"Smiles from the ancients! Look, see that the mighty eyes of your big brother has spotted our catch for today!" shouts Baaku, pointing up ahead toward a shoal of fish splashing and jumping in the water. He quickly turns and grabs his spear, high-kneeing up ahead before he can hear the warning of his younger brother telling him to wait. There is something peculiar about the scene to Kamau. For a moment, a glimpse in his mind has told him that he had seen this happening before.

Whoosh! The spear leaves the hand of Baaku, the older brother, cutting through the air and then making impact with the water.

"You see that!" he calls back to his younger brother, trotting to retrieve his spear. "Fortune is with us, brother, giving me sharp eyes, a swift and powerful thrust, our dinner problems are solved!" Baaku salutes, digging the shaft out of the murky waters to reveal a large twitching river perch. "Brother, have you seen such a fish? Not even Father could deny such a champion prize!"

Experiencing a tentative sensation, the younger brother, Kamau, slowly creeps toward his brother up the river.

"What is wrong with you?" Baaku asks Kamau. "Quickly, bring the line!" he yells to his brother. "Don't be so hard on yourself, little brother. We will get you a catch!"

Kamau grabs the line from the canoe and heads toward his brother, just as amazed at the sight of the perch. From beyond the reeds of tall grass, they make out a grunting sound resonating within the distance. Yet as the brothers take notice that something is not right, the grunting sound is now traveling at a fast pace in their direction. The momentum of whatever producing the grunting sound has made ripples of waves throughout the water. The eyes of the young brothers stretch as wide as the sun. Baaku, the older brother, catches a glimpse of the terror in the eyes of his younger brother, and he manages to spin himself around to witness the emerging of a young hippopotamus bull, charging at a rapid speed. The unpredictable beast is extremely aggressive and temperamental in the protection of his territory. He plows directly at Baaku and gives a swipe of his head, sending the brother into an upended lunge, missing just inches away from goring the boy.

Kamau, acting on instinct of his nature, doubles back to grab his spear, then rushes toward the melee of the massive beast attempting, with its best efforts, to maul and trample the intruding boy.

"Hey!" yells Kamau as loud as his lungs could muster. Trotting over the waters, he thrusts his spear at the hippo. The feeble stick bounces off the impenetrable skin of the dominant creature's body, but this does not postpone the movement of Kamau, who manages to spring his body in between the beast and his brother as he stumbles to gather his footing. Both arms stretched to the skies, Kamau stands there shielding his older brother, giving caution to the wind about his safety. The hippo and boy are locked into an intense stare down. In their pause, it's like Kamau is able to enter the mind of the hippo, and they can understand each other.

"What are you doing in my territory?" demands the hippopotamus.

"Excuse my brother. He can be an idiot sometimes. We mean no harm in disturbing your peace," he responds in his mind.

The fearsome beast lets out a raging, "Get out of my river!" He widens his gaping mouth, the enormous hippo's muzzle extends as wide as both the boys' bodies combined. Kamau instantly has a vision of his head being taken off by the jaws of the hippo; he flinches and shuts his eyes, bracing himself for contact.

Squawk comes from above, and a large water eagle takes a direct dive, targeting the eyes of the hippopotamus distracting him from his victims. The hippo throws his head, sending the eagle into a roll, its body's momentum pulls it into the water. Simultaneously, a strong gust of wind hits the water, and *boom*—a brilliant flash of purple glow sends both boys flying out of the water. Wildly thrashing from within the water, another scarred hippopotamus appears. Just as enormous in size as the opposing bull, but this hippo is noticeable, more weathered with cicatrix tissue and much more menacing in its aggression.

The brothers both try to assist each other in getting their footing. Baaku still has the spear in hand and the perch still ran through lifeless on the end of it. They cannot believe the dynamics of what they are witnessing; it is like the other hippopotamus is protecting them. The siblings both give glances of disbelief and shock; both can read the thinking of the other. *By the cosmos, the ancestors protect us!*

The frenzied hippos are engaged, with maws extended wide and their tusks acted as dueling sabers. Both are searching for any inclination of intimidation from its opponent. Neither is backing down, but there can only be one. This standoff can be endless, or until one of the hippos ends up dead. The beasts slam into each other; the worn hippo pounces from its hind legs. The younger bull is risking a puncture to its blubber. The younger bull slips and gives ground; the worn hippo reloads and snaps it jaws again, landing a decisive bite to the head of its opponent. The ferocious blow to the head brings the competition to an end. Acquiring a nasty gash to its crown, the younger bull wiggles from the grip of the worn hippo and gives his last huff and puff in way of defeat. Exhausted and licking its wounds, the younger bull makes a hasty withdrawal, returning through the reeds in which he came. The worn hippo, in victory, gives charge after the younger bull, ensuring that its opponent has retired.

Thinking better to take advantage of the hippo's distracted attention, the brothers sprint through the water, tossing their spears with the river perch and line back into the canoe.

"We have to get back to the village!" Baaku calls to Kamau, rotating the direction of the canoe. They both turn and head off as quickly as possible to avoid any more conflict, especially with the worn hippo. They want no part of that. With their backs turned from the mix-up between the two hippos, a second gust of wind jolts them back. Again, there's a crack of the wind and brilliant flash of purple radiance. *Boom*—the wave of energy generated from the gale, sends Baaku and Kamau once again off their feet and under water. The brothers, submerged underwater, swiftly stand to their feet, their guards ready from the suspense of not knowing what comes next.

"Hahaha!" With their ears logged with water, they can barely make out what seems like the noise of laughter. Have their ears deceived them? "Hahaha!" The laughter continues. As it carries across the breeze, the brothers begin to recognize the voice from which the laughter came. The two quickly glance at each other as they identified the figure emerging from out of the reeds of tall grass.

"Hahaha! It seems that the big brother has learned that it takes more than his brute strength and might to win the duel," says the angelic-like voice.

Baaku and Kamau both leap with astonishment. "Grandmother Amina!"

The village elder stands strong in her posture, staff clenched in hand. Her skin shines a beautiful bronze, reflecting the rays of the sun. She is also lined with markings of the clan elders. Her hair, was as silver wisps of air drifting on the night's horizon, is braided down the length of her back. Her athletic torso is draped in her traditional clan garments; the entirety of her countenance emits an aura of power and wisdom.

"As my young kings and beloved grandsons have learned here today, there is never a dull moment and never a time to be careless. One must master intellect through understanding. Never antagonize your brother for power lies in various forms. Furthermore, the power from that unity can be a formidable force. There is balance in everything. Rushing forward with strength and power alone without giving care to the opponent or situation can be foolish." She eyes Baaku. "Fear," she says and pauses for a moment, turning away from her grandsons, "fear is a mysterious sensation. It can be a positive or negative stimulus. Fear can lead one to discipline oneself to such harmony. They begin perfecting their craft, ascending their skill level in the cosmic bond to do the most wonderous things under the cosmos. However, fear can also ravish one's mind, filling it with cowardice intent, entrapping it into the voids of eternal turmoil, chaos, and strife. Power and might are displayed in different forms of actions and decisions, like knowing when and when not to strike. A brother's love prompts him to act with no concern of his own life to protect his brother, the most dignifying display of courage." The elder Amina turns back toward Kamau. "Internal and external strengths—the two most important elements of the warrior-mystic. Internal strength— the delicate, the unnoticed, and the eternal. External strength—the outer shield, which fades with time. To take the path of the warrior-mystic, one must travel the road of knowledge and peace, seeking the highest understanding of the cosmic bond. The essential element of the warrior is strength, while the fundamental nature of the mystic is intelligence. The balance of these two elements create the warrior-mystic. Acquiring the interpretation that all things, animate and inanimate, affect each other. All cosmic energies possess a positive and negative counterbalancing force in the universe. The quest for the warrior-mystic is to be in complete balance and harmony with those universal laws of the cosmos, maintaining the balance between the cosmic energies of the mind and body as one. OK," she concludes solemnly, striking down her staff in the water's mud. "Enough for today's lesson. I am pretty sure your mother and father will be searching for you two, wondering where you have slipped off to. There are many tasks that need strong hands to prepare for your baby sister's naming ceremony tonight. I know your vigorous natures will be of great use. But one last thing, one must always be mindful of our brother creatures of the swamp. As you have seen, they can be very hostile when not treated with proper respect."

"Yes, Grandmother Amina," says both the brothers in cadence, bowing their heads in homage.

The brothers have consistently heard of tales of the ancestors' ability to harmonize with their consciousness, and depending on the level of their focus, they can tap into their cosmic energies, and incredible feats can be accomplished. They have known that their grandmother has carried on a strong line of warrior-mystic within her, joined with the feats and deeds of their grandfather's heroic lineage as well. They have listened around the tribe's fire stories of many celebrations, how the mythical efforts of their grandparents standing together in the eye of death, held off fleets and battalions of marauding invaders. They have known that in their youth, their grandparents stood in the highest regards of all the tribes, as the most powerful in the cosmic arts, and they are the last surviving bloodline that has knowledge of and practices all the tribes' known oral traditions and rituals. Nonetheless before that day, they had never experienced that magnitude of the cosmic power. At no previous time have they witnessed their grandmother's transfiguration powers and capabilities. Yeah, she has done things in the cosmic, such as conjuring healing herbs and influencing the elements of water, fire, wind, and earth, as well as telepathically communicating through the cosmic bond. But never anything like this in their twelve and eight years.

"She always says that nothing is impossible within the bond, big brother," Kamau says to Baaku. The two brothers follow their grandmother, as the former matriarch of their tribe, leads her two grandsons through the snaking waterways amid the thick, towering reeds, rearing them back toward the tribe village.

"At least, we still have the perch," mentions Baaku, the boys eyeing and giggling at their catch's carcass.

Later, as the period of dusk arrives, the tribes' village is illuminated with the fires from lit torches and the glow triggered from the beetles of fire's bioluminescence. The village community is in jubilant spirits in anticipation of the naming ceremony's festivities. Droves of the other tribes begin to arrive, making a grand entry. Dancers and musical performers, marching and singing to the beat of drums, displaying banners of the tribes, dressed in dazzling garments of lavish color. Welcoming their kinsmen and tribesmen in warm embrace, the tribe joins in circle, which represented the tribe's unity with the universe. The entire tribe prays, and the opening remarks begin. "Brothers and sisters of the earth tribes, we are gathered once again together in this illustrious moment because we are one being of the cosmos, all connected within Father Universe's cosmic bond."

After ceremonial prayers and welcoming address, the presentation of the family and the baby for the first time to the village is proceeded. The visiting tribes present gifts, prayers, and blessings to the baby. Songs of praise to Father Universe and Mother Earth are performed to welcome new life into the tribes. Elder Amina, the presiding elder, embellishes on a tribal tale of old. Proceeding, she presents items that signifies the path to a fruitful life. She then dips her hand into an ancient tribe concoction of fermented berries and honey and slides her finger across the surface of the baby's lips. According to the nature of the baby's reaction, it is then given its name by the elder.

"Zola!" The baby's name is pronounced by Elder Amina. Next, the name is announced by the family, then the elder council, and finally, by the community. The ceremony commences with drumming, dancing, and eating of foods to celebrate and honor new life, leaving the tribes people to enjoy their time together. The ceremony concludes with the chiefs and tribe elders in council, sitting and discussing events of the outside world with each other for hours into the night.

CHAPTER 7

A DISCUSSION OF BUSINESS OPERATIONS commences between two cousins. "Yeah, li'l cuz, ya'll did good with that last plate of dog food, real good. That's going to make everything with this new deal work out real smooth, showing this motherfucker that we can move this amount of weight in new product at a fast and consistent pace," says the older cousin running down the goings on of the operation. "Since the come down on the pill mills, it's been a bitch trying to find buddies to go to the doctors for prescriptions. Not only that, these bitches are modifying the blues into some gel shyt! But bringing back that old-school *H*, that shyt will be hitting!" The older cousin takes a drag from his cigar and exhales a puff, then passes the cigar to his younger cousin.

Receiving the cigar, the younger cousin takes a drag and puffs.

"So how much money can we make off this shyt, cuz?" asks the younger cousin.

"Li'l cuz, listen to me now. We done pushed a lot of shyt out here. I'm talking from bars to beans to white and to green. We even hit a few big licks. But, cuz, we ain't never seen money before. How we gonna see money with this *H* shyt, cuz. I'm talking million-dol-lar-a-week money, cuz," he explains.

"Damn, cuz, for real?" The younger cousin attempts to process the words he was hearing.

"Yeah, cuz, square business. No bullshit! All you gotta do is keep the li'l niggas in line and get that shyt off, cuz."

The younger cousin takes a drag and passes back the cigar. "So who's the new contact, cuz? You never let me know how you ran into this situation," he asks.

"All you need to know right now, li'l cuz, is that we got power in high places, and they operate in a broad network. We takin' over traps, not just downtown and uptown. Soon, we will be operating out west and down south too. In due time, li'l cuz, in due time," responds the older cousin.

The younger cousin sits in the passenger seat of the car, hooked on every word from his older cousin, and like a good soldier, he is ready to follow all orders by any means. Contemplating on the possibilities on the new business venture, the kinsmen can't help themselves but to smile at each other.

"'Bout to get back out here to my rounds, let ya ass get back to the party!" says the older cousin. The younger nods his head in approval.

At the same time—*Pop! Pop! Pop!*—both the hearts of the two cousins sink as they heard shots ringing in the distance from within the car's cockpit. The two meet eyes.

"Where the fuck is your brother?" the older cousin cries out to the younger cousin. "Go get them niggas and find his ass!" he commands his cousin.

*****

About ten minutes after Iesha has had her run with her upper-classman admirer and dodging the hounding questions from her new associates about if there were any interests in him, she finally convinces her comrades to leave the area that they are hanging to form a search party to locate Ronin and his group of friends. Lo and behold, Iesha follows her nose leading her to the outskirts of a skirmish, and not to her surprise, she manages to find Ronin, dead center amid the ruckus.

"Oh no, Ronin, now what have you gotten yourself into?" Iesha says aloud.

"That's your brother?" the girls inquire in excitement.

Iesha drops her head, embarrassed to confirm, but she realizes that the drama of the scene has sparked the interests and enthusiasm of her associates. Iesha and her associates witness the towering friend of Ronin barking at a restrained boy and then back at Ronin, asking if he was cool. Ronin's towering friend lets go of the boy in his grip. Yanking himself together, the boy barks a few words and disappears in the crowd. Iesha pushes her way through the crowd toward Ronin. As she approaches her brother who is with his teammates huddled around him in discussion, Iesha, not making quite a polite entry, shoves through the pack.

"What the hell, Ronin?" she exclaims, gazing at her older brother.

"I didn't start it," replies Ronin to Iesha, returning the piercing look back at his sister. "Dude came out of nowhere and started swinging at me." He tries to explain.

"Yeah, trouble just always seems to find you," she snaps back. Both group of friends—now looking at the dispute between Iesha and Ronin—are not sure who is acting like the older of the two, with Iesha acting in such a motherly way.

"Bro! Iesha! Ya'll need to calm down. Both of ya'll are heated!" says Paul, stepping in to mediate the situation. "Bro, put li'l sis on beat and let her know what happened," says Paul to Ronin. Next, Paul leads the group of friends away from the debate between Ronin and Iesha.

"Ronin, why do you have to keep up your mess? You keep thinking you are invincible!" says Iesha in a stern manner.

Ronin chuckles. "What do you expect me to do? Just lay down and not defend myself? He came at me!" he contests.

"That's the problem. You defend yourself too well with your fist. You laugh, but it's not a game. You know how things are around here. These guys like to shoot!" lectures Iesha. "I wish you would just promise me not to get into any mess while we are out!"

He realizes that no argument can be mounted up against the truthful statement of his younger sister. "I tell you what! I will promise you this that I will not in any form go out of my way to start any type of trouble. That is the best I can promise. I don't know, li'l sis, there is something in my spirit that just won't let me back down when I am provoked, but I will try, deal?" asks Ronin.

Iesha is aware that getting Ronin to be passive in any such situation is like getting a five-year-old to happily sit for a shot of Novocain at the dentist. So to sway Ronin into taking some consideration of her thoughts without much of a fight, Iesha takes what she can get as a moral victory. "Deal!" Iesha agrees; both she and Ronin seal the deal by a handshake.

Pop! Pop! Pop!—subsequent firing of shots resonate through the atmosphere. Ducking and squatting, Ronin pulls Iesha into his chest, wrapping her, as if he were a human blanket covering the fetus of a baby. The shots send the panic-induced crowd of the party into a scattering stampede, the attendees not knowing which direction the shots were being fired.

"Aaieee! Aaargh!" Sounds of yelling spring out from the trampling mob.

"You good? You good?" Ronin asks Iesha under his cover. Assisting her from the ground, Ronin brushes dirt away from Iesha, scanning her up and down, checking to see if she was hurt during the melee.

"Yeah, I'm fine!" says Iesha, quickly answering back, her hands now shaking from her rattled nerves. Ronin senses the tense hands of Iesha and clenches them within his grasps. A jolt of anxiety hits like an alarm through the body of Iesha; she senses a surge of negative energy.

"Ronin, look out!" she screams, pointing in the direction of an armed assailant barreling down with a pistol aimed directly toward them.

Heeding his sister's warning, Ronin turns to meet the eyes of the shooter. "Shyt!" Ronin yells as he recognizes the hooded young alpha. His orbs glaze with hate and death among the rushing swarm. Ronin understands the intent behind the actions and the gaze of his opponent. It means that there is no returning to reconciliation; his opponent wants blood, his blood by any means. With Iesha's hand engulfed in his own, Ronin clamps down on his sister's arm and takes off in a full sprint, nearly yanking Iesha's arm out of its socket. The teenage terror takes off behind Ronin and Iesha. While in pursuit, he lets off another shot through the crowd, just missing Ronin and Iesha. The bullet makes impact with a wooden-constructed concession stand. The foot chase ensues. Ronin and Iesha run around the block, their heart rate pounding and pulsing like a racehorse. The two teenagers witness what the human body is capable of when in danger. Iesha, being athletically inclined as well, keeps pace with her brother—at some moments, matching Ronin stride for stride as they sprint across the backroads and township of Basin Worth.

A gang of street thugs, shifting on orders from their higher authority, pursues the trail of disorder. They observe the younger brother of their leader in hot pursuit of his prey, and like good dogs, they follow suit and give chase. Mike-Mike, the pursuing assailant, goes berserk running through every nook and cranny of the neighborhood after his victims. The entire locale is an obstacle course of obstructions.

"Fuck nigga!, he screams after his prey in frustration, tearing through lawns, hurdling over fences, and even doghouses too. He fires another two shots. *Pop! Pop!*

Crash! The ricocheting bullet strikes the window of a parked car.

"Ahh!" screams Iesha. Shards of shattered glass cut into the arms of Iesha and Ronin while they used the car as cover. In the time of fence jumping, the older sibling's perceptions are working on overdrive from the rush of adrenaline generated from running for their lives.

Ronin, more concerned with the safety of Iesha and navigating their heavily obstructed route more than the danger of his own life, perceives or hears a voice speaking to him, "The path of the warrior-mystic is entirely about using your surrounding environment." Ronin shakes his head, snapping himself back into focus. He continues to lead in their getaway, keeping himself and his sister moving, but not before knocking over a cluster of trash cans. Ronin then leads Iesha down an alleyway, which he figures will double them back, leading to the block of the party. Wasting no time in making decisions, Ronin keeps them moving. He leads his sister left at a fork in their route. Unfortunately he miscalculates. They come to a dead end. "Fuck!" exclaims Ronin.

"Ronin, I need a second to catch my breath!" exhales a winded Iesha.

"We don't have second!" stresses Ronin.

Iesha bends over and breathes heavily. "I just need a moment!" snaps back Iesha.

"Damn it!" Ronin curses himself in frustration. Spinning in place, Ronin attempts to think quickly in that dire moment. "Iesha, we have to keep moving!" insists Ronin, being aware of the disadvantages of being positioned in the obscured junction. He grabs Iesha's hand, making a U-turn in their route, returning to the forked path.

"Hahahahahahahahaha!"—a delirious and sinister laugh. To Ronin's worst fears, hunched over and laughing in hysterical amusement stood, the young alpha; he laughs and talks to himself as though he has schizophrenia. "I told them I was going to get this motherfucker! Hahaha! Look at this shyt, fucking bootleg Bonnie and Clyde ass nigga! What you got to say now?" says Mike-Mike, wielding the small discreetly carried pistol. "Got a bad li'l bitch. I see what got you actin' all Superman and shyt!" he says, referring to and eyeing Iesha.

"Don't talk about my sister!" lashes Ronin. He can sense the enjoyment of the opponent savoring his upper hand over the unarmed target.

"Damn, don't tell me that. This shyt just might hurt because I'd sure like a piece of that!" He winks and shakes his head, gun aimed at Ronin. Iesha is petrified with the entire scene.

"Say one more thing about my sister, and I'll fuck you up," says Ronin calmly. In reality, the pit of his belly is filled with butterflies of anxiety; Ronin feels the sweaty palms of Iesha. The two combatants lock eyes.

"Hero-ass nigga, come on, fuck me up. I got the gun!" spits Mike-Mike.

Ronin's body or his intuition senses the fight-or-flight situation. Ronin knows there's only one way of making it out of there. He will have to put up one of the grittiest and vicious fights that he has ever contested in against his ruthless assailant.

There is a prolonged silence; a gust of wind blows through the alleyway.

"Well, it looks like it's going to be you or me!" says Ronin, his body tense. "I just have to bet on me and put that aim to the test!" Iesha gives Ronin a bewildered look.

"You're a stupid motherfucker!" says Mike-Mike. "Still talking shyt!"

"If I got to die, I'm going to die fighting!" declares Ronin. He glances at Iesha and back to his opponent.

"Ronin, don't be stupid!" pleads Iesha to Ronin.

"Just be quiet. I love you, and I'm sorry," he says to Iesha.

"Hell, Ronin, you're talking crazy!" says Iesha in a perplexed tone.

Ronin brushes the comment from Iesha aside and gives an empowering smirk to his sister. In a speed game of chess, the clock is ticking with both opponents sizing each other up, daring for one to budge.

A bead of sweat flows down the forehead of Mike-Mike and descends to the concrete, marking the signal of go. Without warning, Ronin quickly shoves Iesha away from his body toward a line of dumpsters.

Pop! A shot is fired as the combatants make their advances. Tumbling upon the pavement, Iesha rolls and discovers herself behind the cover of rusted green dumpsters. "Argh!"

She hears in the distance the muffled groan of Ronin as she lifts herself from the ground.

*****

Bzzrt..."Hello?"

"Tony, I think we just caught up to him. Sounds like he is about a block away!" A street soldier makes contact to his superior while in pursuit.

"Call me when you get to him, and ya'll keep his dumbass there!" orders Tony. The squad leader of the street thugs continues to track the trail of their commander's younger brother, his band of six hounds behind him.

*****

"Argh!" yells Ronin as he feels the hot, burning sensation of his flesh in his left arm. His body's adrenaline works on overdrive; he takes the blow that hits like a locomotive and keeps moving.

"Bitch! Stop moving, nigga!" exclaims Mike-Mike at his opponent's agility, realizing that he is almost out of ammunition in the single-column magazine, and he does not have another. Seven of the eight .380 rounds has been ejected. Mike-Mike dashes toward a staggering Ronin and fires his last round, emptying his cartridge. *Pop!*

Ronin makes a somersaulting dive, just shifting from the bullet's path. *Kraak*—sounds the ruptured pavement from the ricocheting bullet.

"Ronin!" screams Iesha, concerned for her brother.

Ronin rotates and bounces from the concrete posthaste, down in ready position, gauging for his incoming opponent's next shot attempt, his eyes focused.

"Fuck!" the young alpha, Mike-Mike, screams, as he's now out of ammunition. His opponent is far from being incapacitated; it is as though he has been given a boost of energy. An irate Mike-Mike begins to realize that he came expecting to chase down an easy prey, but instead, he has found himself a mortal enemy. He does the first thing that comes to his mind in his state of rage—he chunks the pistol at Ronin.

Sidestepping the .380 semiautomatic pistol, now being used as a projectile, the epiphany hits Ronin that his opponent is out of bullets. Being struck in the arm, Ronin now realizes the turn of events; the fight is now much more evenly matched against his undersized attacker. Blazing like a bat out of hell, Ronin lunges forward, and in an instant, he and his opponent are locked in and engaged with each other. *Wham!* Ronin throws with his limp arm a straight left jab to Mike-Mike's face, busting him in the nose. A returning left hook from Mike-Mike lands on Ronin's jaw. "*Thwack!*" Mike-Mike swings another wild right, widely missing a ducking Ronin, who comes up from his dipped position and lands a straight right to his opponent's gut, including a one-two combination to Mike-Mike's head.

"Motherfucker!" he yells, staggering backward. "Ahhh!" he screams and lowers his head, making a raging charge toward Ronin. Ronin grabs Mike-Mike's crown in a headlock while his opponent hurls wild blows at his stomach and midsection. Ronin attempts to lift Mike-Mike's contoured body, and a sharp stinging pain causes his arm to give out, and both he and Mike-Mike land and hit the ground—*smack!*

Ronin, battling with the spirit of an ancient warrior, is now in a ground tussle with this teenage killer on the block. Drowned out wails and blurs of Iesha screaming Ronin's name frantically—"Ronin! Ronin! They..."—are all he can make out among the noise of grunts. Ronin stands over Mike-Mike, now in a straddling stance, and hears the tapping sound of footsteps coming at a fast pace. Ronin is able to break away from the grabbing arms of his opponent, just in time to catch the sight of the charging cavalry of street-gang members coming to the aid of their struggling comrade.

"Mike-Mike!" hears Ronin from the enraged mates of his opponent. By now, they are in full sprint, nearly on top of his position.

"Ya'll help me get this motherfucker off me!" Mike-Mike whelps, sending out his distress call to his crew.

Ronin, thinking it is better to reposition himself in the alleyway before he is completely flanked, backs away, releasing his hold on Mike-Mike. Distancing himself away from the approaching wave of brutes, Ronin bites down and ready's himself again in a defensive stance facing his challengers.

"Whoa! You done fucked up now, boy!" shouts Mike-Mike, gathering himself from the ground. Revamped from the presence of his backup, Mike-Mike feels empowered once more, wiping himself down as the seven-man crew have their guns drawn on Ronin. Mike-Mike makes way to one of his mates and snatches the pistol from his hand. "Give me that gun!" he orders, returning his aim toward Ronin.

Ronin is to the point of combusting with anxiety as he faces the firing squad. He has had it and is fed up with the toying of his and his sister's lives. So filled with rage from the idle teasing that he can barely focus, he begins to feel dehydrated like he is going to catch a cramp. The same tingling feeling with his forearms and fingertips from his previous Charlie horse attack starts to ache.

"Oh great, not the time for this stuff!" mutters Ronin, cramps beginning to fire off. He gathers himself and takes a deep breath as if in meditation, and the most obscure thing happens.

A voice, carried across the wind, says to him, "Through the cosmos, nothing is impossible."

A spark is set off inside Ronin, which rekindles his fighting spirit. Prepared to make his last stand, he speaks to his assailants. "I don't want any trouble, or for anyone to get hurt, but if you want all my rage and my pain"—he pauses to inhale and exhale—and once more, with a raging bellow, he says, "Then take it!"

A hurricane-type gust of wind hits the alley, and an implosion of electric energy comes from the body of Ronin, knocking back the group of attackers. At the same time, an explosion of the electricity surges throughout the back alley, bursting streetlights and building windows, also sounding off nearby car alarms.

Stunned and confused, the attacking party in the alleyway staggers trying to recollect what has just happened within the past ten seconds. Ronin—now drenched in sweat, winded, and heavily breathing—cannot make sense of what is going on with him. Iesha, still taking cover behind the rusty green dumpsters, is now a mute witness to whatever just happened.

The band of eight street thugs aimlessly drifts back and forward, now unarmed. Their weapons and all objects of metal substance not weighted or rooted to the ground are now magnetized to the front sides of the dumpsters. Shaking the cobwebs of confusion from their equilibriums, the gang regains their focus to mount an attack.

"I don't know what the fuck just happened," says Mike-Mike, "but we are getting in your ass tonight!" dashing toward Ronin with his gang of brutes. The battle brawl commences.

Iesha, not being able to contain herself to the sight of Ronin being outnumbered, enters the brawl, jumping on the back of one of the battling combatants. Ronin is electrified by the aid of his baby sister. Her actions of putting herself in the line of danger sends a sense of urgency through him. Ronin displays an insane mix of hand punches and acrobatic kicks, like some martial artist. Ronin keeps his converging attackers at bay using knees, elbows, and whatever limbs he can use to defend himself. Iesha, clinging to the back of her opposition, swipes and claws at his face, scalp, and shoulders; causing Iesha's victim to buck her like in a Texas rodeo.

The vaulting contestants stumble, colliding into one of the rusty green dumpsters. *Whaam!*

From within the dumpster, twisting and scurrying, out leaps a long mammal about the size of a medium dog, but it has black fur on most of the under portion of its body. On the top half of its body, from the peak of its crown to the tip of its tail, stretches a band of white fur. The animal scurries and then pounces on to one of the gang members, freeing up Ronin from another attacker. The fearless beast is relentless with its thrashing behavior and menacing obscure growling—*rattle, rattle!*

The hysterical goon shrieks and runs into a wall and knocks himself cold. The dodgy creature pounces again, contouring its body and scurrying at rapid speed, looping in and out, up and down the battling gang members, sending them all into squeals. "Aaiiieee! Eeeyaaa!"

Then suddenly, from among the chaos—*poof!* A burst of wind emits an emerald-green glow, imploding a cloud of dust from the wall of smoke.

Kaboom! Whooosh! Smaack!

"Ouch!" knocked from within the smoke cloud, a goon hits the pavement with a thud.

Thump! Whoosh! Pow!

"No!" out comes Mike-Mike, flying and making an impact on the concrete. "Angrrr!" he yelps.

As the cloud of dust begins to clear and disperse throughout the alleyway, all members of the attacking street gang are all down on the ground, rolling and cowering in pain. Iesha, also down on her hands and knees, coughs, attempting to clear her throat. She raises her head to the view of a hooded figure wielding a staff, standing and giving leg support to a heavily breathing and battered Ronin.

"Cough! Cough! Cough!" Iesha heckling while on all fours trying to gather herself from the ground. From the pavement, Iesha mutters to her brother, "Ronin!" her voice still a bit weak, her eyes fixed on the hooded figure in possession of her bleeding and battered brother. Still coughing and inhaling fumes of cloud dust, she almost gags. Iesha pushes herself from the cold, damp pavement. "Ronin!"

she says a little louder and clearer. "Ronin, how are you?" She speaks now on her feet.

Ronin—bathed in sweat, heaving, and grasping for air—is barely standing, crunched over with the aid of the hooded figure.

"Ronin! Let him go!" she yells, staggering toward Ronin and the mysterious individual. Moving closer, Iesha notices the bloodstained jeans and T-shirt, causing her to rush to Ronin, tackling him from without of the hidden person's support. Ronin collapses onto his sister's shoulders. His weight takes them back to the ground. "Damn it, Ronin!" exclaims Iesha, taking Ronin's arm from around her neck. Beside herself from the sight of blood, she frantically searches over Ronin's torso.

"Are you all right? Are you okay? Ronin?" Iesha bombards him with questions.

Ronin, clearly not in the best shape, can barely respond, still gasping for air and grunting in pain.

Another gust of breezing wind carries a voice, which whispers within the ears of Iesha. "A sister's love is the gateway to all impossibilities!" The peculiar voice carried on by the breeze startles Iesha, but not giving it much attention, she continues to tend to her brother while the hooded figure circles the pair.

"Ronin, oh my god, say something!" says Iesha as she shakes Ronin.

"I'm OK. I'm OK," he responds. "Argh, my arm!" he exclaims in pain.

Iesha, now examining the gash in her brother's arm, breaks into tears and covers her mouth. Iesha focuses on the thought of how she can help in repairing Ronin's wounded arm. She places a hand just hovering over the gash. Tears, running down her face, fall on the wound, and Iesha's hand and a developing glow of golden illumination discharges from Iesha's palm. Under the glow of light, Ronin's tissue and skin begin to bind and reconstruct itself, mending tissue and skin and sealing over into a keloid wound.

Ronin looks at his arm and then to his sister, who is just as speechless as he is about the whole episode. "Yo! What the hell is going on?" he says, both he and Iesha wearing blank faces.

"By the cosmos!" exerts the hooded figure to what he has just witnessed, pulling back the hood to reveal a bearded and dreads-headed man. He looks as if he were someone's well-fit grandfather. "Quickly, young ones, we must be fast in our movement," says the bearded man. Both Ronin and Iesha turn to look at the unknown man who has aided them.

"What? Wait!" shouts Iesha, once again, rising from the ground, dirt—and gravel-ridden. "Who are you, and what is going on? We can't just leave with you!" protests Iesha, wiping herself. "There is much to explain and still much to be manifested, but this is neither the time nor place to discuss it!" says the older gentleman.

"Seems like a perfectly good time to me!" snaps Iesha. "We get shot at and chased! My brother has some kind of seizure that causes an electrical shortage! There are rodents the size of dogs jumping out of dumpsters, transforming into someone's grandparent! And not only that, I start to her voices and, glowing with light, heal wounds! I think it's a perfectly good time to say something!" she demands.

"The only thing that I am at liberty to share with you at this present moment is that, it's due to your will to act and other various qualities. By the blood of your lineage and the fighting spirit of your ancestors, you have been chosen, young ones, as champions by the ancestors who speak through the cosmic bond," he explains.

Ronin gathers his bearings, rises from the pavement, and recognizes the bearded elder. "The guy from this morning!" he gasps and drops his jaw.

"Yes, my young friend, this is not our first time running into each other," he says to Ronin.

"You know him?" a confused Iesha questions Ronin.

"Yeah, yeah! Remember the older gentleman I was telling you about from the bus this morning?" says Ronin.

"Yeah," replies Iesha.

"Well, this is the guy!" states Ronin.

Police sirens now alarm the city's streets; the gang of street thugs lay in the back-alley streets winded and in pain after their ambush has been spoiled in an obscure episode of supernatural events. The surviving victims, aided by an unknown gentleman, now offered to guide them on their route.

"Young ones, please quickly we must hurry. All will be explained," says the older man. Having enough action for the night, they accept the older man's offer with little resistance, especially after Ronin recognized him from earlier that morning.

Mike-Mike finally gathers his wind from his breathtaking land on the pavement. He scans the scene to see his fallen comrades incapacitated and his victims gone. "The fuck!" he utters to himself, trying to gather his equilibrium. Lying next to Mike-Mike, piled up in a heap, are the handguns of the thugs, demagnetized in a mound of metal clutter, and on top is his .380 semiautomatic. He grabs it from the pile. Hearing the police sirens in the distance, Mike-Mike springs from the pavement, and in his moment of drama and selfish cowardice, he abandons his comrades, taking off down the alleyway.

Minutes later…

Screech! A dark sedan pulls to a stop; out jumps a bewildered Tony. "What the fuck happened?" questions an irate Tony, observing the scene of his crew helping one another to their feet. "Buck, what the hell happened? I thought I told you to call me when you saw Mike-Mike," says Tony to one of his comrades.

"My bad, bro, but when we caught up to li'l bro, Mike-Mike was getting jumped by a gang of niggas! So we had to jump in and help li'l bro get them niggas off him," explains the thug.

"Where's Mike-Mike at now?" asks Tony.

"Bro, you know li'l bro, after scrapping them niggas took off, and li'l bro got up flexin', grabbed his fire, and went chasing after them niggas!" responds Buck.

"Ya'll niggas get ya'll sorry asses up before 'trol gets here! We need to find this crazy nigga before he gets into some more shyt!" declares Tony.

*****

An itsy-bitsy spider creeps above, in the alley's corner, observing and giving audience to the skirmish in the city's streets. Pleased with the cinema, the reclusive, slow-moving brown spider energetically scales its web, ascending the side of a two-story office building. Upon reaching its summit—*vrroom!*—a flashing loud noise and streaming fumes carried as a smog cloud travels in the winds of the night sky. High above the city, the shapeless mass of floating vapor soars the horizon of bright lights and traffic. Clear across the county, the smoke appears to make its descent.

The smoke cloud makes impact on the pavement, creating a fissure of brimstone. Appearing from the smoldering chasm is a man of slender build, dressed in black leather pants, biker boots, and vest with no shirt, exposing a tattoo of a fiddle on his back. With a causal countenance of a man, he strolls, taking a drag from his cigarette, and steps through the doors of a business establishment that read, Illusions Gentlemen's Club. Giving a nodding gesture, he slides by the door man and cashier.

Bump! Bump! Bump! The sound of music grows louder as he advances through the corridor.

"Handful of grease in my hair feels right, but what I need to get me tight are those—girls, girls, girls!" the rock band Motley Crue pumps throughout the club's main room. Navigating in the dimly lit area, bypassing the stage of parading dancers sashaying and enticing customers, and scanning the room, he spots his man—semiformally dressed in vest and tie with clipboard in hand. He approaches the club's back bar.

"Fiddleback!" the man behind the bar bloats, throwing his hand up in the air. "What brings you here? Creeping out of the shadows of cracks and crevasses tonight on the hunt, eh?" says the husky, dark-haired gentleman behind the bar.

"Oh no, how I'd love to play with the kittens, but there is no time for pleasure. Evening, Donovan!" salutes the one called Fiddleback.

"No play, huh?" says Donovan.

"I am here to seek an audience," responds Fiddleback.

"An audience? With whom do you seek this audience, if it is not by the company of my girls?" inquires Donovan.

"I would like to speak to him!" says Fiddleback.

"Him?" says Donovan.

"Yes, him—Lord Chaos. I know he is here," replies Fiddleback.

"Well, this must be some rather important amount of business. As you know, he does not like to be disturbed with nonsense while he is breaking in the new inventory!" states Donovan.

"Believe me, Donovan, my boy. No amount of inventory could ignite his excitement like this jewel!" says Fiddleback.

Donovan guides Fiddleback into the club's private chambers, away from the main halls. Donovan triggers a hidden button that reveals a secret door. The passageway is arcane in fashion; it leads to a case of descending stairs. "Fiddleback, this could be news for the ages!" says Donovan. "If what you say is true, a warrior-mystic and that magnitude of cosmic energy displayed has not been seen in almost sixty-plus years!"

Moving downward into their catacomb environment, they see thousands of inscriptions dressing the passage's walls. The stairways conclude the access to a large candle-lit room, decorated with paintings, statues, and ornaments. Most of the items identify with immortalizing death or depicting scenes from ancient wars in history. The ceiling-high doors are designed with an engraved portrait of onyx boarder in gold. Donovan propels the massive doors ajar, Fiddleback at his rear. Lined in silk satin sheets, a mattress to put a California king to shame, fully indulged in the company of three young ladies lay a man.

"I have been anticipating what you will do to me!" says the gray-haired man, entangled in his huddle of women.

"Excuse me, my liege!" announces Donovan. "Pardon the interruption, but we have news!" says Donovan.

"Another issue about the girls in transport? Have the negotiations not been settled?" inquires the older man.

"No, sir, all things are going on that situation. But our friend here, Mr. Fiddleback, has news on sighting a mystic and potential pupil," explains Donovan. Vaulting from the pile of women, the man tucks in his shirt and adjusts his suspenders. "You have news of what? Tell me!" his eyes grow blazing red, and the cynical smile on his face stretches from ear to ear.

*****

Bzzrt…Bzzrt… "Hello…"

"Ronin? Where in the hell are ya'll? We have been riding around the block in circles the past twenty minutes looking for ya'll! Are ya'll cool? Are ya'll straight?" the voice of Paul answers the line, running his mouth a mile a minute with concern.

"Bro, take a breath. We are OK. Just had an adventure in that getaway. Some of the strangest things happened that I can't even explain, I can't even understand it," says Ronin, still winded. "But we found some help, and they agree to escort us back toward the party," says Ronin.

"Bro, 'trol got that place shut down," replies Paul. "We are in the car now, so just let us know where you are now, and we will come scoop you up."

"Bet!" answers Ronin, looking for their location at the next junction of street signs. He gives their location to Paul.

"Be there in a minute!" confirms Paul.

*****

"Now, my young ones, you are safe for tonight, so go home and rest your heads. There is no need to stress yourselves anymore about what has happened here this evening, for tomorrow brings a new day. And as you can see, your lives will never be the same again. Things have been revealed to you tonight that transcend beyond the capable understanding of the most-studied man," says the elder. "All will be explained in due time. The ancestors have already begun to manifest themselves to you. What matters now is that you both get your rest and restore your strength. There is much to prepare for, and mind, body, and spirit must be in prime condition for what lies ahead."

*****

Thirty minutes later, north across town…

Three teammates ride home from a party. "Damn, that shyt was crazy! That party was like on some real gangster shyt!" says Matt.

"Mad crazy!" injects Mike from the back seat, "like some stuff out of Grand Theft Auto."

"Haha! Bro, ya'll sound like a move dawg!" Laughs teammate Big Dee. "But that shyt was bananas! Talk about a way to spend a Friday night after ending the season last night, crazy!"

"I sure hope Ronin and his sister are OK," says Matt.

"I'm sure they are all right. Ronin knows how to handle himself. He ain't no punk. Paul is going to hit me anyway when they link back up," states Big Dee.

Blip! Big Dee's cell phone receives a text message. He opens the message and reads. "See, that's him right there," announces Big Dee.

"They found them, and they are on their way to the crib!" explains Big Dee.

"Cool!" responds Matt.

"Bro, just pull up and drop me off right here at the corner store," requests Big Dee, pointing to the twenty-four-hour convenience store on the adjacent corner. "You can just drop me off there. I need to run inside, and I can walk to the crib from there," says Big Dee.

"Dude, you don't have to walk, man. It's not a problem for us to wait," replies Matt.

"Bro, it's all good. The crib is right up the street, and plus, I might check out the avenue before I go in," says Big Dee.

"You sure, bro? It's not a big deal to wait," asks Matt.

"Bro, I got this. I'm Big Dee. What's going to happen to me?" says Big Dee.

"All right, bro," says Matt, pulling into the store's parking lot.

"You sure, you good?" asks Matt once more.

"Bro, I'm good, good," says Big Dee.

The teammates clap hands in salute. Next, Big Dee hops out of the car of his teammate Matt, and Matt drove off into the night.

En route to his apartment complex from a night outing with friends, Big Dee makes his journey down a hidden path that acts as a shortcut from his apartment complex to the main road, where the store is located. Approaching a breakage in the chain-linked fence, Big Dee is unaware of the watching stalker who aims to use its prey's own web to lure it in.

Swisssh! Something within the bush startles Big Dee, making him jump and look. The bushes shake. "Must be a racoon or possum!" says Big Dee to himself. Shrugging off the noise, he continues walking.

The stalker watches as his prey is being played like an old fiddle, steps from behind the bush, pouncing in full stride. Big Dee pivots and turns, but it is too late to react to the handgun being aimed at his torso. His hands raised, he stares down the gun's barrel of his assailant.

"Ride with that nigga, die with that nigga!" are the words uttered by this hooded attacker.

"Bro, it ain't even like that—"

And before Big Dee could finish his sentence—*pop*—a shot to his torso. *Pop! Pop! Pop!* With three more shots to Big Dee's torso, he falls in a slump to his knees, taking a heavy gasp. *Gaaassp!*

The assailant neither feels nor shows any remorse. His feelings are dead. He places the pistol to the side of Big Dee's head. The assailant then squeezes the trigger once more—*pop*—firing an accurately placed bullet to Big Dee's brain, causing him to gasp no more. The attacker dashes off into the night.

CHAPTER 8

"Brought to you now, a live Breaking News Report from PBC News!"

"As she enjoyed her time partying with family and friends at a block party in the Basin Worth area, a fifteen-year-old girl was struck in the head by a stray bullet. Kameshia Blackwell was pronounced dead around 11:45 p.m. on Friday night at a local hospital, according to local reports. Blackwell was shot around 10:45 p.m., Friday, in celebration of a friend's birthday at a block party held in Basin Worth, said police.

"Witnesses and attendees were having conversations, enjoying music, and dancing when an altercation between two young males had interrupted the party. The situation was thought to be settled and resolved. Therefore participants of the party continued. About fifteen to twenty minutes later, a hooded assailant opened fire into the crowd. Blackwell was reportedly struck while running in the stampeding crowd. Paramedics rushed her to a nearby hospital in critical condition, where she was later pronounced dead.

"The sophomore reportedly is an honor student and member of the color guard team at Blanche High School. Police are looking for any information on the people or person responsible. A $5,000 reward has been offered on the case," PBC News reports.

*****

"A shooting in Northeast Providencia late Friday night left a young man fighting for his life. The victim was shot five times. Just after midnight, police got an anonymous call bringing officers to 1500 block of Pines Avenue. Officers found a man in a wooded area.

The victim was face down, suffering from gunshot wounds to the chest, stomach, and head. Investigators said one of the bullets was discovered in the man's right temple.

"'Paramedics rushed the man to St. Mary's Hospital in serious condition. He was not carrying any identification, so the name and residents of the young man is unknown,' said authorities.

"Detectives said that they are unaware of what the shooting stemmed from. Police do not have a suspect's description, and they tell us at this moment they are not getting much help from the people living in the shooting's area. 'A bullet recovered from the scene was like that found at the location of the shooting death of Kameshia Blackwell,' said Sergeant Jake Leblanc, spokesman for PBC police department. 'However, even though believed to be related, no connections have been confirmed in the two cases, which remain under investigation,' the police said. Kimberly Mercer reporting live, PBC News."

*****

Police chatter and static on a radio…

Cruising up to a congested crime scene, homicide detective Charles Toussaint jumps out of his patrol car.

"Detective Toussaint!" expresses a saluting uniformed officer, marking off the area and supervising the scene.

"Early enough for ya?" says the officers.

"Talk about an all-night hustle," replies Detective Toussaint. "Damn jurisdiction pulling me in right before I call it quits! And goddamn favors for the DA. I hate election years!" spats Detective Toussaint. "The new assistant district attorney is adamant about gearing up a new task force to put out on the streets, this being his first string of multiple homicides. So what do we got?" asks Toussaint as he and fellow officer canvass the area.

"We got an unidentified male, shot five times. The body is in there!" says the officer, extending his arm and pointing toward a hidden pathway.

"Got any evidence restored?" asks Detective Toussaint.

"Not sure," responds the officer.

"What do we know about the scene?" asks Toussaint.

"Male was face down on arrival, no known witnesses to any altercation. As you can see, the location is well covered. Looks like the victim was taking the path as a shortcut into the apartment complex, and as he was walking, he got ambushed, or he and someone got into an altercation. Either way, it didn't end too well for this guy. The attacker fired multiple shots. We got the call of shots being heard," explains the officer. "Blood splatter here and here. No visible footprints so far."

"I got something!" shouts a crime-scene investigator from the brush.

Detective Toussaint rushes over toward the crime-scene officer as he used a pair of tweezers to pick up a spent cartridge shell from within the gravel.

The officer examines the 120-grain bullet. "This looks to be the bullet that traveled with so much speed and power causing the fatal injury," states the officer.

"That's the same type of bullet that killed Blackwell," says Toussaint. "Fucking animals! The same type of bullet," he mutters once again to himself.

"Got a mother that has been calling into the station since about five o'clock this morning, saying that her son had not made it home. She is down at the station waiting on a positive ID at the morgue," informs the uniformed officer.

*****

In a brightly lit room, accented with cold, surgical steel equipment, sit two women in embrace. One woman is slightly older than the other.

"Mama, I know he went to a party with his teammates last night. But I called the boy Matt, and he said that he had dropped him off at the corner store last night around 11:30 p.m., and he went home. I know they use that pathway to get back and forward from the house to that store. Nobody has said anything yet!" says the younger woman, panicked and sobbing.

"It might not be him," says the older woman. "We still have to wait to get in the back, so we don't know."

Escorted to the back, the mother could barely feel her legs; the feeling was surreal. The detective leads her into a room; he then draws back the covers, revealing the cold, blue-faced corpse stretched on the table.

To her worst fears, "That's him, that's my son!" She breaks down.

*****

"I believed I felt a surge of energy tonight!" says Lord Chaos from his possessed human host. Dark energies of his rank can easily inhabit humans whose spiritual and mental transplant had been successful, keeping them imprisoned from what was eternal and what was masked as such. "Thought it was just from the excitement of my new flesh pets, aren't they lovely?" he rambles, referring to his harem of women. "But if the report of what you have seen, Fiddleback, is true, a reading of this magnitude has not been felt since the 1960s. We must locate this boy and his sister, and unmasking this unknown staff-wielder is most eminent. After thousands of years of the human species being blinded behind the veil of agents manifested by their negative cosmic energy, it's damn near impossible for man today to know who their true enemy is—man's emotion imprisoned in the firmament filled with a millennia worth of vengeance, hate, fear, and resentment. This could be the final blow in bringing the years of manipulating and toying with those emotions to its final demise. There is no need for any champions of hope stirring up the pot in their attempts of enlightenment. The long-lost ancestors' string of meager victories will soon come to an eternal end. This boy—he has enemies, yes? Seek them out, and we will use them in wreaking havoc in the name of evil, tipping the balance in cosmic forces. This will be most pleasing to the master," says Lord Chaos.

*****

Rumbling thunder...a storm is brewing. The crush of storm clouds, shapeless and massive in size, filled with thunderous lightening, send explosive cracks and clatters as it approaches at rapid speed. Its wave engulfs the horizon line of the city. Ronin awakes to a pounding headache, laid out on his living room sofa. His body feels as if it had been run over by a southbound freight train. Parallel to him, stretched out on the love seat knocked cold, is his sister Iesha, with her mouth hung open in deep sleep.

Ronin's head feels like scrambled eggs; he sits up and grabs his head, attempting to suppress the pounding sensation. "What the hell happened last night?" he utters to himself, trying to recollect on the previous night's events. *Was it a dream? Had something been slipped into his drink at the party?* he thinks. Ronin looks over his shirt, remembering it to be torn, dirty, and stained with blood. It is now clean and stitched as if fresh out of the store. *Could it be a dream?* The aching pain in his body proved to tell a different story; he grunts leaning back on the couch, lifting his shirt to examine his sore arm. Ronin is astonished by the keloid wound confirming the exploits of the night previous. Ronin quickly grabs the t.v controller and clicks on the television, turning to the news channel.

"As she enjoyed her time partying with family and friends at a block party in the Basin Worth area Friday night, a fifteen-year-old girl was struck in the head by a stray bullet," says the news reporter.

The alarming news sends tingling jolts throughout Ronin; he immediately calls out to Iesha, shoving at her to wake up. "Iesha! Iesha!" he calls, saying, "Look at this on the news!" Iesha, barely awake in a stupor, tries to wipe the eye boogers away. "A girl got hit by a stray bullet last night at the party," he exclaims, turning up the volume. "That's crazy!" says Ronin.

"Blackwell was reportedly struck while running in the stampeding crowd," continues the reporter.

"I've seen her around before," says Iesha.

"I don't think I knew her," replies Ronin, both siblings' eyes glued to the television.

"The unidentified body of a young man has been..." the news reporter says.

*Bzzrt…Bzzrt…Bzzrt…*Ronin gets a call, he reaches for his cell phone vibrating in his pants pocket. He reads Paul's name across his phone's ID. "Hello?" he answers.

"Bro, I've been blowing you up all morning!" The hysterical voice of Paul roars through the phone.

"What's up, bro? What is it?" asks Ronin.

"It's Big Dee. The police found him dead. He had been shot!" The quivering voice of Paul sends Ronin's body into a flush.

*****

12:30 p.m., Saturday afternoon

Providencia Beach County police department—inside waits an anxious Ronin, tapping on the cold steel table in the department's interrogation room.

Tic! Tic! Tic!—the hands of the wall clock overlapping Ronin's tapping. In walks two detectives introducing themselves.

"Detective Muiz," salutes the older, heavyset man about a head length shorter than his younger counterpart.

"Detective Concotti," salutes the other. He takes a seat across from Ronin, taking out a pen and notepad. "Understanding that this is a difficult time for you and your friends, we just want to ask you a few simple questions that require simple answers," explains Detective Concotti.

Ronin breathes to poise himself, focusing through his roller coaster of emotions.

"So what time would you say you and your friends arrived at the party?" asks Detective Concotti.

Ronin braces himself as he gathers his response. "Erik and Paul picked up my sister and I from the house around 9:15 p.m., so I believe it was between 9:30–9:45 p.m. that we got to the party," he answers.

"Witnesses at the event said there was an altercation between you and another guy. Can you tell us about this?" inquires Detective Concotti, taking notes.

Ronin goes into a detailed synopsis of his day's encounters with his assailant, starting with that morning on the bus, and, unfortunately, bumping into each other at the party.

"And you had never seen your assailant before that day?" asks Detective Muiz.

"No, never before yesterday, and if I had, I didn't know it," Ronin responds.

"And shots were fired right after this tussle?" asks Detective Muiz.

"I wouldn't say right after. Maybe twenty minutes after. I was talking to my sister. We had put our minds back to the party," he explains.

"If you were to see the assailant again, could you recognize and identify the suspect?" questions Detective Muiz.

"Yeah, I could," replies Ronin, having flashing visions of the menacing eyes of the young alpha engraved in his memory. "And I think that I heard that they call him Mike-Mike."

Detective Concotti raises an eyebrow and jots the alias in his notes.

*****

Ting...ting...ting...ting—the recurring jingling of pocket change and housekeys of a nervous Paul, who's tapping his leg uncontrollably, him now in the position of being questioned in the interrogation room.

Tic-toc—the clock hands overlap with the jingle of Paul's foot-patting.

"When was the last time you saw Melvin Davis?" questions Detective Concotti. "We had just met back at our teammate Matt's car, after running from the shooting," explains Paul. "We had lost track of Ronin and Iesha while everybody was running. So we had figured we try to split up and find them. After about ten minutes of looking, Matt and Erik started to panic from the sirens and everything. To keep them from bugging out, Big Dee and I figured that I would just call him when I found Ronin. So Big Dee, Matt, and our other teammate Mike took off. I guess that had to be around 11:00–11:15 p.m.," replies Paul.

"The guy that your friend Ronin had gotten into the physical altercation with, do you know him? Have you seen him before?" asks Detective Concotti.

"I can't say that I know him," says Paul, presently with beads of sweat forming on his forehead and his hands clammy. "Just heard of him before."

"Do you know his name? Or the name of anyone that he maybe associates with?" inquires Detective Muiz.

"No, I'm not sure who he hangs with, or his name. I just hear what floats around in the streets, but I never heard too much on him," says Paul.

"If you see this guy again, could you identify him?" asks Detective Muiz.

"I think so," replies Paul.

"You think so?" repeats Detective Concotti.

"I'm not sure," says Paul.

Detective Concotti jots down in his notepad.

*****

2:45 p.m., Saturday afternoon

Outside of the police station, Ronin, Iesha, and Matt, distraught over the news of the death of their teammate and friend, wait for Paul as he goes through the question-and-answer procedure. This is all too real to be true, the teens feel, trying to catch hold of the reality of the situation or gain comprehension to understand the situation. All are silent as they patiently wait on Paul.

The sight of Paul appearing from the doors and climbing down the stairs of the police station produce the first sign of life in Ronin since he received the unfortunate call that morning. In an instant, Ronin is upon Paul at the midway point of the stairs to discuss the information shared with the detectives.

"So what they say? What you tell them?" rushes Ronin in his questioning.

"I told them what happened at the party," says Paul.

"Did you let them know that you knew who the dude was?" asks Ronin.

"I didn't tell them I knew him. I told them I heard about him around the streets," explains Paul.

Ronin understand the culture of most individuals who live in the neighborhood of, not being most trustworthy of the police, and having the label of snitch tied to your character is not a good look either. Therefore, Ronin feels the need of Paul to be vague a little in his answers. But he cannot understand why Paul would withhold any information that will lead to catching the guy who might possibly have done this to their friend.

Why hadn't Paul just said what he told him about the guy? This infuriated Ronin. He snaps and lunges in a charge at Paul, snatching him up by his shirt. Ronin can only think of the loss of his friend. "Why didn't you tell them who he was?" he exclaims to Paul. "Why didn't you tell them, bro?" Paul's shirt in a tight grip.

Paul, grasping at the forearms of Ronin, attempts to release his hold. Iesha and Matt converge on the boys in a huddle to break up the two.

"I didn't tell them because if I put him in the mix that would get me tied into it, and if Mike and his people go down, that would mean I go down too!" shouts Paul, struggling from Ronin's hold.

Ronin, perplexed by Paul's word, releases Paul's shirt in disbelief, trying to make sense of what Paul was saying. Did this mean he had something to do with or new something about the death of Melvin?

*****

"What do you think?" says Detective Concotti, as he and his partner, Detective Muiz, walk through the police station.

"Think the brother, sister, and teammate Matt are sincere in their stories, no masking anything in their stories, just emotionally screwed up by the mess. And by the way, if this guy they are talking about is one of the few Mike-Mikes that we know, then they should be nervous," says Detective Muiz.

"That friend of theirs, Paul, seems a bit skittish, like he is holding something back, got some more he wants to tell but just won't say. But like you said, if it's one of the few Mike-Mikes that we are talking about, he is within good reason to not talk either."

The chatter of police conversations and phones ringing overlap throughout the station.

"Hey, Detectives Muiz and Concotti, Captain says he wants to see ya in his office as soon as you got done in interrogations!" says a fellow officer, as they enter the processing and intake area.

"Did he say what it is about?" asks Detective Concotti.

"Not a clue, but I think something on the new case," says the officer, throwing his hands up in the air.

*****

Ring...ring...ring! "Hello?"

"Hello! This is Captain McCain speaking!"

Detectives Muiz and Concotti step into the office of their superior while he is in conversation. They patiently take their seats as the captain gestures with his fingers, asking them to excuse the phone call.

"No, he hasn't made it in here just yet, but my two guys just got in here," says the captain as the two detectives eavesdropped on the chatter. "I am going to give them the rundown now and get back to ya. All right later!" He slams the phone and folds his hands, looking at the two detectives. "Due to this election year, the Special Assistant US attorney of Florida's southeast division has called for the formation of a special task force between the homicide and narcotics units of the two involved townships since tying evidence leads to suggest that the two crimes maybe linked to each other," explains Captain McCain.

Both Detectives Muiz and Concotti take their seats. Fixing his coat, Detective Concotti asks, "Are we not taking the lead on this case? If not us, then who?"

"Everything you got on this case and get on this case, you are to report to Detective Charles Toussaint. He should be here any minute," said the captain. "Guy's been on the force three years. It's said he knows the streets up and down, and he worked them too."

"Ahh! Captain, come on, you got us reporting to some new suit!" exclaimed Detective Concotti.

"Hey, it's not me! This case is crossing jurisdiction. The case was picked up by the big guys, so it's not me. This guy was handpicked and brought in on this to not make things complicated and stir up the pot. Collect your facts and evidence, report what you find to Detective Toussaint so that we can find this guy, and he can present what is discovered to the grand jury and close this case out," says the captain.

Knock! Knock! Knock! Someone taps on the office door.

"Come in," replies Captain McCain.

The door swings open, and in pokes the head of another detective.

"Gentlemen! Gentlemen!" he says.

"Detective Toussaint, I presume," says Captain McCain, standing to shake the hand of the younger athletically built detective.

"Yes, yes!" says the detective, returning in salute.

"Detective Toussaint, I would like to introduce you to our two lead homicide officers who will be working with you and the other members on the task force—Detectives Muiz and Concotti."

*****

Because if they go down, I go down!…If they go down, I go down! I go down! the words of Paul's last statement echo in the back of Ronin's mind, unprepared for and confused with Paul's decision to withhold information from the detectives about his combatant. *Why would he not be willing to give all the information he knew on the guy that potentially took the life of our friend? Didn't he care?* Ronin thought to himself. Pulling Paul away from the ears of Iesha and Matt, Ronin asks. "Paul, what did you mean when you said if they go down, you go down? What did you do?"

Ronin and Paul have been best friends since the sixth grade, and that's an understatement. They have been more like brothers. They let each other know about everything they have going on—good, bad, or the ugly. Well, that's at least what Ronin thinks.

Ronin reminisces on one of the first moments that he and Paul had become friends in their middle school gym class. At the end of gym class, the guys headed into the locker rooms to change for class. Ronin noticed a frustrated Paul sitting in a corner of the locker room, Paul's face planted into the palms of his hands as if he were about to cry. Ronin stepped to his flustered classmate and asked if he was OK. Paul proceeded to tell Ronin that he had placed his bag into a locker without a lock and that someone had went into his bag and took his money for lunch. Ronin empowered by the spirit of justice went into immediate action, imposing his size and aggression on every individual in the locker room. After the strip search and speech from Ronin, Paul's twenty-dollar bill reappeared on a bench in the locker room before the bell rings. Ronin and Paul had become inseparable in getting into capers with each other since that moment.

Ronin is ready to hear Paul's explanation behind his statement before he got so upset. Paul is hesitant in his posture, but he knows he can no longer stall; Ronin will not accept anything less. Following a moment of prolonged silence, "Paul, what are you talking about?" questions Ronin again, sounding a lot calmer in his tone.

Paul takes a deep breath and says, "Bro, you remember a few weeks ago right after the Pine View game when I skipped practice because I had an emergency?"

"Yeah, I remember that," replies Ronin. "What's that got to do with this?"

"Just listen to me, and I'll get there. A few weeks back after school, I had EA run me back to the house real quick before practice started to check on my little sisters and brothers. I run inside, and when I get there, the lights and water had been cut off. I knew Ma had said that she would be a few days behind on the bill payment, but I was not expecting my li'l brothers and sisters to be sitting in the dark. I couldn't leave them there like that. I told EA to let Coach know that I had an emergency and had to miss practice."

"That's why Coach sat you out of the first half of the next game!" injects Ronin.

"That's why he sat me out that half!" repeats Paul, reconfirming Ronin's statement, and he continues, "But hold on, let me finish.

Anyway, there is a faucet outside of our complex building that turns on, so I'm walking to fill up buckets of water to boil and flush the toilets. Guess who sees me?" asks Paul, hitting Ronin with a light jab to his chest.

"Who?" inquires Ronin.

"Tony, that's who!" says Paul ecstatically. "He was out in the hood posted up, just chilling with his crew."

Ronin remembers Tony from middle school. The kid has always had the flare to live fast and has an infamous reputation that follow him—being affiliated with and related to a major player in the crime world. Ronin had few interactions with Tony while in middle school besides the pickup basketball games before and after school. Not only that, Tony was also one year ahead of Ronin and Paul.

"So as I'm filling up the buckets, Tony sees me, and he calls me over to him. He asks me, 'What's up?' So I let him know about the whole lights-and-water situation at the crib and my momma coming up short. This nig' Tony pulls out a band of hundred-dollar bills and hands me three of them. Then gives me a party pack of his to sell on front. He told me to get my money and get back with him when I get done and needed to reload," explains Paul, feeling like a ton of bricks has been lifted from his soul. Ronin, feeling his friend's pain and sensitivity to the subject, doesn't continue with the bombarding raid of asking why Paul didn't say anything to him or to Coach. But Ronin is far from crazy. Deep down, he knows why Paul hasn't said anything about the situation. Ronin knows the helpless and embarrassing feeling of being without and of wanting help but dare not asking for it. Ronin is just thinking of a few years ago when their lights had been shut off and he had brought Iesha to practice with him so that she could complete her homework. It killed him to explain to Coach what was going on at home, putting his family business out in public.

"But that's what I mean when I say if they go down, I go down! If I were to let the detectives know that I knew who he was, that would lead the investigators right to Tony and his crew!" says Paul.

"I've seen Tony three times since then to load up!" says Paul, informing Ronin. Ronin sighs and places his hands on his hips, now understanding the complexity of Paul's situation.

"You think letting them know who this guy was would have anything to do with that?" asks Ronin.

"That's exactly what an investigation would lead to, bro!" says Paul. "You know how information travels in the hood. Somebody already knows we are here. Either way, if something happens, that's my ass too!"

Ronin is upset about the death of his friend but knows the words of his friend Paul also to be true. The pain of Paul's statement sting like a sharp pain in his chest. Ronin almost fainted, his mind focused only on the task of getting justice for the murder of his friend and threatening their lives.

"Paul, I don't know what kind of situation we have gotten ourselves into this time, but we have to find a way to get out of this mess!" states Ronin, turning to his friend. On both sides, Ronin and Paul are knee-deep in it, and they have to figure the best way to maneuver around the neighborhood psychology of "loose lips, sinks ships!" Faced with an impossible task, Ronin thinks it best to save any more chastisement on Paul.

"Paul!" says Ronin.

"Yeah, bro, what's up?" answers Paul.

"If we live through this, remind me to kick your ass for being dumb!" says Ronin, now walking toward the car of teammate Matt.

Riding home from the police station, Paul gives information on a meeting that is scheduled for that evening. Paul is expected to be there. Paul gives Ronin a brief overview of how active he has been involved with Tony's operation.

Back at home, after being dropped off by Matt, Ronin and Iesha sit in their living room with their mom. Iesha lays her head down on her mother's lap, as Keisha rubs her daughter's head and loosens the braids in her hair. Ronin kicks back on the love seat, staring at the blades of the ceiling fan while they spin. He's thinking of the failed attempts in convincing Paul to not show up for that meeting this evening. Paul thinks it is not a good idea to not show up, believing his absence would be an obvious flag to Tony that something is wrong. Coming to a truce, Ronin does persuade Paul to take him along with him to the meeting as his assistant, if Ronin promises not to let anyone know. Paul just had to wait on a phone call to receive the time and location of the meeting.

"That's why I've been telling ya'll. Ya'll have to be careful out there and around here when ya'll go out doing stuff," Keisha says to Ronin and Iesha. "Ya'll say I try to baby ya'll too much, but look and see, these people out here are crazy! Stuff just does not make sense. Kids can't even go to parties anymore, and you say you didn't know the boy, Ronin?" asks Keisha.

"No, Ma. I didn't know who this guy was before yesterday," answers Ronin. "I bumped into him and his crew yesterday morning on the bus route to school. I stopped the guys from making jokes on an old man. We exchanged a few words, but nothing happened, so I didn't think much about it, and I went on about my business and to school. Small world—just so happens last night at the party, the guys and I are in a conversation. Next thing I know, someone bumps into me from the crowd. When I turn around, guess who it is?" recounts Ronin. "Ma, I don't know what else to say. I was minding my own business. I just stood my ground."

"Yeah, I know," says Keisha. "You have always been a little hot-headed and stubborn, like your daddy! Don't get me wrong. I know you don't start too much trouble. You are quiet, always thinking, and like to keep to yourself like me. It's just something in you that makes it hard at times for you to back down from challenges or authority, whether the outcome be good or bad." She sighs. "My little warrior! And your sister here, always running behind your butt no matter the situation," says Keisha, lightly pinching the nose of Iesha.

"But seriously, are ya'll all right? Are ya'll hungry? Do ya'll want me to cook something before I have to get ready for my event tonight at work? Iesha, did you still want to come? Or, Ronin, are you OK with takeout tonight?" asks Keisha.

"Oh dang, the charity and exhibit's grand opening is tonight! I forgot about that," says Ronin.

Keisha works as a curator and exhibit designer at the county's museum, overseeing various collections in specific fields and periods, along with assisting in planning the layout of the display of items. The past six months she has been working nonstop in preparation for the grand opening of the new exhibit in reverence to ancient Ethiopian civilization dating 3100 BC to 2181 BC. Keisha has really been flustered behind this project. She wants everything to go according to plan. The exhibit is heavily funded by the police department and other city officials in support of the urban youth's historical education program. Tonight's event is an auction hosted by the police department, students and artists from local urban communities donated artwork and performances to auction at the charity event and presentation of the museum's new exhibit.

"Nah, Ma, I'm OK. I couldn't eat now if I wanted to. Maybe I will be able to get something down later. And besides, you have a big night tonight anyway. You should get all the rest you can. No need wasting your time in the kitchen stressing about me, Ma!" says Ronin.

"It's not a waste. I'm just making sure that you and your sister are okay," states Keisha.

"I'm all right, Ma," says Ronin, trying to reassure his mom that he was okay, even though he is going completely bonkers with his thoughts. But he dared not try to explain to his mother what he and his sister had just experienced within the last twenty-four hours. Ronin doesn't even know where to start.

Iesha is in a silent gaze as she lay on Keisha's lap, her eyes fixed upon her brother, Ronin. "Yeah, Ma, I'm fine too," Iesha responds in a nonchalant tone.

"OK, if ya'll say so! But ya'll got about two hours to change your minds before it's time for us to start getting ready to go!" informs Keisha. "Iesha, did you still want to go?" she asks.

"I don't know, Ma," responds Iesha.

"You better hurry up and make up your mind, girl," says Keisha.

Ronin, feeling a rush of claustrophobia coming on, asks Keisha if it is OK if he goes outside to the courts.

"Ma," says Ronin, "do you mind if I go to the courts?"

Keisha gives him a look of concern and pauses. "Umm, Ronin, I don't know with all this stuff going on," she says.

"Ma, it's just up the street," responds Ronin, pleading.

Keisha, in protective mode, wants to refuse and keep her children inside, but she knows that the courts has been a place of refuge and peace to Ronin. The past four years of Ronin being involved with basketball and the dedication to perfect his skills has brought his temperament to a place of balance and tranquility. And to deny him of that at this moment will crush him. "Boy, I guess, better you at the courts playing ball than running around the city causing trouble," replies Keisha.

Ronin moves to head out the front door. Iesha jolts up after Ronin to follow. "I'm coming too!", she says.

*****

"Bet! Bet! Bet money! Bet money, my nigga!" A rowdy game of craps is in progress by a group of men somewhere in a dilapidated warehouse. Across the room, Tony and his cousin Duke sit in a four-way game of dominos.

"You hear from, li'l cuz, yet?" asks Duke.

"Nah, I haven't heard a word from him, and nobody has seen his ass since last night at the party!" answers Tony.

"We need to find his ass. Did ya'll see the news this morning? The whole city's hot. I know li'l cuz is not all there in the head anyway, and when he gets on them beans, ain't no telling what he will do. This li'l nigga gonna fuck up the plan of operation with unwanted attention," says Duke. "We are about to make a major transition in the game. We are in the middle of the process with everything happening now."

Bzzrt! Bzzrt! Bzzrt! Duke's cell phone gets a hit. Cutting his words short, he answers, "What it do?"

"The shipment will be in at 9:00 o'clock p.m., Port of Providencia Beach, dock number 19. Everything with the couriers and customs are taken care of. Have your boys on point. Don't need any slipups on this. And uh, I'll see you tonight at the banquet. Oh, and remember to wear your suit and tie, eh!" says the voice on the phone.

"Yeah, I got it covered," replies Duke. *Click*—the phone conversation ends, and Duke goes in to inform his soldiers on the details of his phone call. "Touché, you gonna take the lead tonight on pickup," says Duke.

"The drop coming in at 9:00 p.m. at the Port of Providencia, dock 19. You and the crew need to be there around 8:30 p.m. Everything with security is handled," he further explains. "Tony, until that time, you and your li'l niggas need to keep looking for Mike-Mike. Gotta find that li'l nigga!" Duke instructed.

*****

Bump! Bump! Bump! Bump! The beat of a basketball hitting the pavement as Ronin dribbles up the street on his way to the neighborhood basketball courts.

"Ron, wait up!" calls Iesha after her brother, now in a light stride trying to catch up. Without a word, the two walk up the street, Iesha keeping an eye on Ronin as he sets his gaze ahead. The neighborhood is docile for a Saturday afternoon. A couple of the courts are occupied by a few grade-school boys, playing a game of twenty-one and just shooting around.

Claiming a vacant court, Ronin dribbles to the free-throw line with Iesha trailing behind him. She stops and stands, positioning herself under the hoop of the basket. She looks into the face of her brother.

"What are we going to do, Ronin?" asks Iesha. "Is all this real? Did all of that last night with the guy in the alley really happen? Why didn't you say anything to Ma about it?" rambles Iesha emotionally.

Ronin sets his form at the free-throw line and takes a shot. *Thuud*—the ball hits the front end of the rim.

"I can't even understand what just happened and listen to you. I am in just as much shock as you are. I was there with you when it started to get all *Twilight Zone*, Iesha," responds Ronin.

Iesha steps and catches the ball falling from the rim, then returns a bounce pass back to Ronin.

"Bad enough Ma's stressed out with work and her event. She is already pushed with traveling to the game this week. She is nearly two steps away from having a heart attack about our involvement in this whole shooting escapade. Big Dee dead!" Sighs Ronin, releasing another shot. *Whooosh!*

"What do I look like now telling Ma or the police about the homeless man that I met on the bus yesterday morning. 'Hey, Ma, this guy I just met came popping out of a dumpster in the form of a large rodent and transformed back into a man doing martial arts and casting spells.' Then we can just explain to her that she no longer has the need to worry about me getting shot or major wounds because your hands now start to glow with some kind of healing light. And let's not forget whatever type of seizure that I had that resulted in an electrical shortage and blackout in the area. I don't know what the hell is going on with us!" exhales Ronin. "But I do know, if we go around telling Ma or anybody that story, we might as well go to Baker's Act and lock up ourselves!"

"I know, Ronin. All this mess is crazy. I can't even register what is happening, let alone make someone else believe it. But we have to do something, and I'm really scared, Ronin!" stresses Iesha.

Ronin does not know what they are going to do or what to do at that present time. But what he does know is that he has to get with Paul as soon as possible and see just how far Paul has gotten himself involved with Tony's crew, and try to talk some sense into Paul before he is in jeopardy of losing another friend.

"Paul has a way to find out who this guy is or maybe where he is. You are going to go with Ma tonight to the auction, like you planned to. But there is a meeting tonight that Paul told me about, and he has to be there. So that means I need to be there," says Ronin to Iesha, who is now beside herself.

"Ronin, don't you think letting the police know would be better? You know, just staying out of the way and letting them do their jobs?" protests Iesha to her brother.

"What do the cops know? They have no clue, and you hear how these street thugs operate. We'd be dead and gone before the cops even know it! And there is obviously something going on around us beyond our understanding. So the idea of just sitting around like bait doesn't sound OK to me. I'm not looking for someone to save us," contests Ronin. "I have to find out for myself what's going on. I can't go off anyone else's judgment. They haven't lived the past forty-eight hours through our viewpoints. They wouldn't understand."

"It's just two dope boyz in a Cadillac"—the tune of the OutKast ringtone alarm on Ronin's phone plays out—"It's just two dope boyz in a Cadillac…"

"Paul, bro, what's up?" answers Ronin.

"Just got the call, bro, with the time and place," says Paul.

"Did anyone mention anything to you about the shooting or Big Dee?" questions Ronin.

"Nah, bro, nothing besides the normal hood gossip. When I talked to Tony, he didn't mention it, even though he did sound a bit aggravated. A part of his reason is that they are still looking for Mike-Mike. Nobody in the crew has seen him since the commotion at the party last night. Good thing about it is that people around the city already know us as being partners, and I was not there when you and Mike-Mike got into a tussle," Paul explains. "But about tonight, we have to be up at the Port of Providencia Beach by 8:30 p.m.," says Paul.

"Port of Providencia Beach?" repeats Ronin.

"Yeah, bro, tonight comes the arrival of a big shipment of new product, and we are on for pickup duty," informs Paul. "Think you can get a ride over?" he asks.

"My mom has an event tonight that she and Iesha are going to. It starts around that time. I'm sure if I hurry and get ready, I could get there. I may be able to catch the bus," says Ronin.

"Bro, whatever you do, you better put a move on it if we are going to be on time and pull this off," says Paul.

"All right. Bet, bro, let me get on it. I'll text you when I am on my way," says Ronin.

"Cool, bet!" replies Paul.

"I can't believe you are even thinking of going through with this, Ronin!" cries Iesha. "I know you have this mindset thinking that you are harder than a rock, but dang it, Ronin, this is by far the craziest situation we have gotten ourselves into!" she says.

"I won't doubt you on that or take that away from you, Iesha. This is some pretty crazy stuff, but guess what?" says Ronin to Iesha.

"What, Ronin?" she snaps.

"I was never able to fire thunderbolts out of my ass before this situation either!" he says to Iesha in a humorous tone, attempting to lighten his sister's spirit.

Iesha quickly responds to Ronin by slugging him with a straight right into his chest and says, "I hate you!" Iesha then breaks into a light snicker before releasing a floodgate of laughter, unable to contain her emotions. Iesha knows her brother's spirit to fight to the very end in what he feels is right. "Ehhh! What am I going to do with you, Ronin?" says Iesha, tilting back her head, looking toward the sky. In her peripheral vision, she catches the silhouette of the large bird from the previous morning. Iesha snaps her head, placing the large bird in her view, and she points. "Ronin look!"

Ronin whips his head around to see what has caught the attention of Iesha. And clear in his sight is the large bird of prey perched atop a roof of an apartment building, its gaze set on Ronin and Iesha, glaring right at the them. The pair of siblings are hypnotized by the soul-piercing eyes of the bird.

"Iesha, do you think that's the guy?" asks Ronin, tapping the arm of Iesha.

"I don't know, Ronin, but let's sure as hell try to find out," replies Iesha.

"Heyy!" screams Iesha at the bird. "Don't just sit there and stare at us. Why don't you come down here and say something? Give us an explanation or something!" she yells, lunging the basketball toward the bird, but the ball fell well short of the bird's distance.

"Iesha!" yells Ronin after his sister. "Iesha, calm down, stop acting crazy now and putting on a scene," he says, making it clear to Iesha that her rant has drawn the unwanted eyes of passersby and the boys playing pickup ball in the yard. Iesha takes a glance of the surroundings and pauses to restrain herself. "I'm sorry, Ronin, but if that is the guy, he needs to say something. He has answers. He has to know," she cries.

"Iesha, I know, but it's no guarantee that, that is him up there. We can only hope, seeing that he did help us, and making a big scene about it in broad daylight wouldn't help anything. Our best bet is to just make it to the house and get ready for tonight. We don't have much time, and I still have to go run the gauntlet about getting a ride to Paul's, cutting it so close to start time of the auction," says Ronin.

"Whatever, Ronin, let's just get out of here. That thing is really beginning to creep me out!"

Ronin and Iesha begin to exit the courts. Ronin and the large bird lock glances with each other, and as if Ronin could hear the bird speak to him in his head, a voice speaks to him, "As long as one remains and stands with the spirit of no surrender and no retreat, all is not lost in the fight." And as if finishing its statement with emphasis, the massive bird gave a mighty *squawwk* and flapped its powerful wings, propelling itself into the horizon of the sun descending behind the city's skyline.

CHAPTER 9

AFTER 750 YEARS OF PEACE, the centralized governments and institutions introduced by the first pharaoh of Egypt, Menes, in the first dynasty had always collapsed by the end of the sixth dynasty. The line of great leadership had been followed by weak pharaohs of hate and greed. The wealth that poured out of Ethiopia had blinded the pursuer of empires and builders of civilization. They did not dare to grasp or understand the human heart and spirit and how key these aspects play in the foundation of unity and devotion.

This era would begin 141 years of anarchy in the motherland. Civil relations and war had become more intense as the larger and more powerful provinces began to force other weaker tribes into a state of national unity. Empires and clans stayed in disorganization and chaos. Civil war had spread over the kingdom and its provinces that had once stood of great achievements. It was said that seventy kings had ruled in seventy days as a result of civil unrest. Rebellions of different provinces seeking independence from weak rulers in Ethiopia had become the thing of the day, an event that the Eurasian settlers had been patiently waiting for a long time. What happened during this period of political chaos would progressively change both the ethnic character of the lands of Africa and Eurasia.

If remembered correctly, since the unification of the two lands of Lower and Upper Egypt, light-complexioned tribes had the right to travel and settle in black Upper Egypt. And despite the general oppositions of mixing the races, there had been a continuous flow of infiltration from the start. What had started out as a small number of people spreading out into the lands and becoming essential parts of life, not causing any alarm. Eurasian settlers began to form communities; some married into families of local villages and became chiefs themselves. Eurasian penetration and expansion in the motherland became normal, which inevitably increased the number of migrating and settling Eurasians.

At this time, humans had passed about eight thousand years of African and Eurasian intermingling of the races. The most significant changes in the racial character of Mother Africa always happened during periods of crisis. The fall of centralized government from Memphis allowed Lower Egypt, which was a predominately Eurasian region, to become independent again. The two-way intermingling and warfare was a victory for those of light complexion when the conquering armies came from their various homelands. Some fought alongside their African nationalists, but majority sided with their native armies. Egypt and the motherland of Ethiopia had become more and more white and light in complexion. Becoming a part of the power elite of the conquerors, not only did Eurasian settlers capture and took control of political and economic power by force of military power, but they also began to, in fact, claim to be from a higher civilization, creating the myth of being a superior creature.

Roughly seven hundred years had passed since the unification of the two lands on the west coasts of Africa, and the process of transforming men of dark complexion from men to half-men had begun. The Afro-Asians were the new breed, which promoted devotion to Asians and hatred of Africans. Africans or Asians would no longer be called Egyptians even though they had been called so since early times. Now if Asians were unmixed, they were called Asians; and if Africans were unmixed, they were Africans or Ethiopians. The breed of Afro-Asian alone would be called Egyptians when in the earliest of time, black would have meant Egyptian, then it fell to blacks and Afro-Asians. White Asians were never called Egyptians even when they ruled all of Egypt. History would follow suit of this classification from ancient times to this day. Those of African title who lost their self-identity by destroying the roots of their past caused the people to lose crucial links with their history and the things of the earth from which the people drew strength, inspiration to move forward, and the purpose of being a human. So the futile attempts to replace his own values with those of a man with a lighter complexion, the dark-complexioned man lost his own personality, and therefore, almost absolutely, he had lost his manhood.

Attempting to sway and appease invaders in self-preservation and self-interests, some chieftains of small villages freely gave their daughters and other desirable females as gifts in exchange for fire-arms, given strategically to certain kingdoms and chiefdoms seeking to become big, wealthy powers and expand their territories over weaker villages. Invaders came knowing that in the pursuit of resources and riches, many Africans became as brutal as the invading Euro-Asians in dealing with their own kind, capturing millions of prisoners to be enslaved or executed in the process.

With the demand for resources and slave labor, this would lead to a built-up animosity, giving birth to a never-ending warfare among those considered Africans themselves, creating an everlasting hatred among varied groups, and destroying any basis for unity. Most importantly, warfare would keep them so blinded and forever hating and fighting one another that they would forget their real enemies.

Invaders neither understood nor wanted to value the culture of the Africans. They were only concerned with exploiting the land for its resources. The lust of the world and lure of wealth had turned them away from cultural truths. Hundreds of years of ravaging the land of Ethiopia by foreign incursions, Eurasian states divided up the motherland for themselves, establishing colonies that ignored the natural and historical divisions of race, culture, and religion. The course that had set the way of that era to maintain structure of the day was through colonization of the mind, pressing the issue, by any means necessary, that the white man is a better human than any black man.

The transplant of the dark man's mind had been a successful operation, having them to deny their African heritage was the easy way to survival. To not do so would be giving up opportunity to life itself and cutting to the direct line to fortune, power, and fame that only Eurasians were able to secure. Black agents, usually those of mixed Euro-Asian and African heritage, were the secret weapons of the new masters of the motherlands. It was a staggering phenomenal accord—the blacks were more ready to fight and die for the cause of the white man than they cared to fight for their own. The motherland's spirit was conquered by her very own forgotten brothers and sisters, jealous of each other—dark complexion against light complexion—tricked into being against something they did not understand. This led to the unfortunate spilling of black blood, which further darkened the pages of history. Conquerors trained strong black armies to hate, kill, and conquer other blacks who were not deemed profitable, productive, and civilized.

None of the conquering powers were established in humanitarianism; they never cared for the native people or trade. Their aim was to create a colony and control the resources. The trend of sacrificing one group of people for the success of another would leave a permanent stain in the history of man, and a fact that would be forgotten by modern society. The successful invasion of Eurasian forces was just an introduction to the era of imperial and colonization incursions, which would change the physical aspects and characteristics of the world and what was remaining of the human nature of man himself. Building a lifestyle and labor habit—that would most certainly lead to the destruction of the entire earth and its inhabitants. The energies manifested from the lust and passion for death, wealth, and power would most certainly tip the cosmic balance, if man had achieved his dream at the expense of all people.

"*Hahahaha!*" a sinister laugh was cast across the abyss of space, as the master of the voids and embodiment of negative energies gave witness to the given results of his millennia of scheming and manipulating man in his feud against Father Universe. His ultimate plan was to tip the cosmic balance of energy within the universe, therefore causing the collapse of the entire solar system by creating a blackhole. The dark entity was a powerful manipulator of negative energy, shapeshifter, and creator of illusions. He had perfected the art of preying on man's desires and took possession of weak individuals who were unprotected by the bond or spirit guardians.

The master of voids could not bear the notion of Father Universe placing the earth children above him, and giving them souls and a place in the universe. The dark entity felt that the humans were playthings and should be treated as such, in its vendetta of rebellion, it aimed to devour the souls of men, leading their life essences into the eternal abyss. Pushed to the side from Father Universe's grace and left in the abyss of the voids, it felt without purpose. The entity conjured and controlled the negative energies of the cosmos, sending agents of chaos and minions of destruction, starting a war among cosmic energies that would stretch across the millennia in stalemate for the human spirit. But the menacing entity was very clever; it had studied and experimented with the behavior of man through the centuries, picking up on their tendencies, and it had discovered that man's belief in one supreme being created in the image of himself and in life after death had made man submissive.

The pursuit of physical wealth and self-preservation was a sufficient method to deceive and destroy the children of earth, setting forward a course that would result in Father Universe's children of earth to forget the language of the universe and its true essences of peace, love, and harmony. No longer able to communicate with the universe or the land, the children of earth would fully lose their honor in the understanding of manhood, which had come with the identity in the pride and connection that had come with the bond. Master of voids' minions and agents preached the gospels of hate, keeping man who had forgotten the language of the universe and earth focused and fighting over various differences, brother and sister of the earth no longer. The hate emitted toward Father Universe and his precious blue orb, Mother Earth, from the dark entity was determined to prove that the unknown to man was fearful, and what men envied they destroyed.

"This is absolutely astounding—the faces of Father Universe and his Mother Earth's children of love. Bahaha, they burn land and destroy themselves in a race to the extinction of each other. With energies of hatred and death, portions of earth children were wiped from the existence and blotted out of the histories of man. How could he love them best? I'd rather the stars burn out and bring down the universe before they be placed above me. Monkeys calling monkeys, the fools will never understand that it is not what's on the outer appearance that matters. It is what is within that appearance that matters. But don't worry, Father, I will make them plunder their faiths into the depths of the abyss!" said the entity. "Shame on you, Father, for not telling them how it works. Although eternal, the universe is in a constant state of change. True energy is neither good nor evil, positive nor negative. The universe is consisted of both because it is both. Yes, Father, we are one. Good and evil only exist in the nature and action of one's heart. The energies that man produces manifest energy particles, as do all creatures of the earth," it explained.

"It is really quite simple to understand. That is the grand ol' thing about dear, oh Father. He just loves to leave out the most important parts of the instructions. The energy that one puts out is the energy that one gets backs. Gone are the days of man when the word *king* meant 'a leader of action,' and the king led from the front of battle, and not from miles away, cowering from the destruction he started. Thousands of years will pass, and the illusion of wealth and military power will be sufficient to guarantee security and permanence," it said. It then summoned the entities of three agents of deception, ranked in the dark entity's highest order.

"Sire, they are coming!" said the energies in salutations. "Grand right on queue. Now it is time to wipe out man's universal power to lead other men and make them lose their value to fight for self-respect, over worth's of wealth, and have man voluntarily give up such respect, having them to forever look at themselves through the eyes of judgment and contempt!"

In 2176 BC, the age of bronze would be marked by days of chaos. Centuries after the unification of the lands of Egypt by the pharaoh Menes, the motherland of Ethiopia had fallen into a complete state of anarchy. For those in a position of power, sleeping with one eye open had to be a well-mastered skill because treachery and the overthrowing of kings were an everyday occurrence.

A pompous figure, with an inflated ego as if knowing everything there is to know under the sun, and whose air breathed with every bit of greed and corruption, plays host to his younger cousin and his troops, who has just taken over the reigns of his uncle's kingdom. With the start of the collapsing centralized government of Egypt in the sixth century, his father and uncle had migrated to the mother country of Ethiopia from Persia. They raided and plundered villages and small chieftains, as lieutenants of a small army of marauding bandits. The uncle, who was the elder of the two brothers, was granted lordship of a few provinces as a reward for his exploits and the loyalties of the bandits being with him. The younger brother was also granted a few provinces, and the charge of one of the most important caravan trade routes, an outpost that had connection between the motherland of Ethiopia and Eurasia. The uncle was an astounding military tactician, and his brother had a prominent mind in the field of trade. The two brothers' skills compensated for each other, and they would settle in the lands of Ethiopia, growing their empires and business ventures. They both intermingled and indulged in the daughters of Ethiopia and birthed sons; first was the younger brother, and next the older brother five years later.

But those days had passed, and the brothers had grown old and died passing on their legacies onto their sons to continue to grow their lineages. It was a grave time in the motherland, and the struggle for power was all too real. The motherland had been split into eight kingdoms, with all the crowned kings claiming to be pharaoh of all of Ethiopia. The younger cousin at that period had just inherited one of the strongest armies in all of Ethiopia, and the older cousin operated with an iron fist as he oversaw the coming and going of every merchant operation traveling through Africa and Eurasia.

"Many things have changed since the reign of your father, cousin," said a man of arrogant stature. Flaunting his "I'm a big deal" personality, as he strode through the halls of his local manor, engaged in conversation with his younger cousin, a humbled spirit who had just been handed the command to a large army and kingdom.

"Can't you see it, Aspurta? There has never been a better time for the dynasty of our lineages! The legions have never been stronger. You can now complete your father's dying wish and become the true king of all of Ethiopia!" He celebrated.

"I know, Gatura. I hear you. I am just so tired—tired of the politics and treachery and the continuous wars between the provinces. The whole damn of it is a drain!" said the king solemnly. "Do you ever get tired of the news of war, Gatura?" he asked his cousin and paused. "I just cannot help but think of my mother and of the stories she used to tell me when I was a young boy. Do you remember those stories, playing as young boys? Father used to say those tales were mumbo-jumbo African stories that should be paid no attention to, but I loved those stories they always humbled me. I often think of the days of great pharaohs such as Menes and when he first unified the lands of Egypt. It had to be a grand time. Now just imagine if only I can be as grand a leader as him," he stated.

"Bah, cousin, this is no time to think about tales of tortoises and spiders. Those are children's matters. My father never let my mother speak of that rubbish. It is time to grow some backbone, Aspurta. You have to prove your might and show you are here to earn your title and crush your enemies. Without any notion of a weak king, that is not a good look. Without haste, you must take control of the chaos and put back the pieces to the puzzle of the broken kingdoms. Ideas of peace are just that—ideas. It is no time for that now, cousin. Military might and power must be the way to take what is yours. But tonight, put that out of your head, little cousin. Oh, excuse my manner, my king, excuse me! Tonight, your legions and you rests your heads in my company, enjoying the best flesh of women, food, and wines across the lands. Enjoy yourself tonight, cousin. Think not tonight, leave it till tomorrow!" said Gatura, leading his cousin through one of his estates as he entertained the king and his soldiers as honorary guests at a hosted party.

Hours later, Gatura hobbled and stumbled around his main entertainment hall, resulting from a belly full from his indulgence of fermented yeast and berries. He manhandled his way into conversations with anyone who could bare to listen to the man. He thought he was quite the catch with the ladies. A mysterious guest at the gathering showed a peculiar amusement in conversation with Gatura; he brought to his attention three women who were anxious to meet with him and fulfill his fancies.

"Very womanly, very womanly, I see!" commented Gatura on the figures of the ladies. "And they have all their teeth, makes the kissing enjoyable when I have my way!" savored Gatura in his slur of speech.

Moments later in privacy, Gatura could hardly contain himself from keeping his hands off the women. "I'm sure that what has you excited to see me is that you have never had the pleasure of being in company with a man such as myself," he said, full of himself. Too busy in the sipping of wine and groping, Gatura's desires of flesh had weakened his senses. He never noticed the sly hand play of the women, as they wooed into his ear and manipulated the movement of his body.

"We really should not be upset with you. We already know. All you men wants are all the same," said the women.

Clink—the sound and feel of cold iron closing around the wrists of Gatura.

"What? What is this?" he said, in a confused manner. Wrestling in attempts to free himself, Gatura fixed his gaze on the three women who had seduced him. "What is the meaning of this?" he demanded.

The women just laughed and danced around in circles in a trancelike state. Gatura's yelling was futile, as he was weighted down in chains. He began to feel dehydrated; his eyes started to blink rapidly; his vision was obscured. It must be because the women whom Gatura had seen now were not women at all. Gatura had begun to see glimpses of demon entities that had taken form as women.

"Dying to meet you and fulfill your fancies!" The three demon-entities sang and continued to dance in circles. It had become clear to Gatura that he had been trapped in some type of an illusion, but it was too late. He thought he had been lusting in the flesh of women in one of his private quarters when, in reality, he was bound in chains, locked in someone's dungeon.

Gatura was tortured for a period. The demon-entities toyed with his flesh, ripping and tearing it apart in a frenzy of snarls and growls, casting agonizing pain upon Gatura, which had mirrored the darkness in his heart. Just on the brink of death and in excruciating pain, a dark entity came to Gatura, speaking of things it would show him of the world. The entity told Gatura that his knowledge of the earth and universe did not even scratch the surface. It promised Gatura things like power, riches, and eternal glory—everything that Gatura had ever dreamed of. All he had to do was serve the dark entity's purpose and bring him the sacrifice of man's flesh that had turned away from the image of the god of man. The entity promoted that

Gatura, not his cousin, Aspurta, should be king of Egypt and all the motherland of Ethiopia and become a god. The entity told Gatura that it could make that happen for him and show him the way. The entity told Gatura that it could just patch him right up and send him on his way to glory. Or he could cast his essences into the eternal abyss so that he could live out the past few hours of his life as an everyday eternity. The dark entity whispered a plot to Gatura about murdering his cousin, Aspurta, and overthrowing him. It convinced him that it would take only one man to get into his chambers and kill him and that man should definitely be someone he does not suspect would kill him. The dark entity had made that offer over a thousand times to over thousands of men and women across the millennia

Later, Gatura walked into the private quarters of his younger cousin and king, escorting three beautiful women. "My dear cousin, as I have said, indulge in the night and let the mysteries of tomorrow come!" said Gatura. "I was just dying to introduce to you these three lovely young ladies, who have been so excitedly intrigued to fulfill your heart's desires!" said Gatura with a sinister smile.

*****

"Raise the alarm! Raise the alarm!" alerted a legion guard. "Run!"

Tingle, tingle, tingle—the sound of horns and bells calls for an early rise to the estates' guests.

Stomp, stomp, stomp—footsteps of armed soldiers quickly running into the quarters of a sleeping Gatura. Arising from his sleep, the startled Gatura asked, "Captain, what is going on?"

"My lord," said the captain, "we need you to come with us immediately. We have an emergency. There has been an accident with the king!"

Later that afternoon, a legion of soldiers marched into the market square of a caravan trading post, where business was being conducted. The soldiers carried and posted signs and banners that offered a reward for any information on the death of the king, or the murderers. Also, merchants and traders were told that any information on people of ancient practices and culture would bring an enticing fee.

*****

The winter winds were upon us, and the time was here for that season's group of young boys from the tribe to prepare themselves to test their skills and responsibilities to earn the right and title to manhood. Boys from the tribes would also discover who would be chosen with the calling from the ancestors to walk the path of warrior-mystics. In early times, children of earth had acute senses and other various abilities according to their cosmic vibration and connection with that bond. Heightened reflexes, a sense of supernatural forces and presences, and intuition were just a few common abilities capable of those connected with the bond.

According to stories told by tribe elders, when connected to with the cosmic bond, warrior-mystics could tap into an abundant source of cosmic energy, allowing some warriors the capabilities to manipulate the elements of the earth, enhance their strength and stamina, perform healing tactics, as well as other abilities, considering the warrior's concentration level. But over time, the world grew and man lost the language of the land and cosmos and began to speak the tongue of hate and destruction. Most all, children of earth had forgotten they were beings of the cosmos and had lost their abilities, and the few remaining tribes that kept up with the culture of the ancient ways, not every child of the tribe could wield the bond. Few tribesmen inherited those abilities, and they were recruited as apprentices to become warrior-mystics after they had completed their spirit trials. But no one with the calling was forced to train as a warrior-mystic; it was just a calling that could go unanswered if one chose not to walk the path of the warrior-mystics. It took a tremendous amount of meditation and concentration to control it. Warrior-mystics were taught by his or her fitness to comprehend and learn. Many children of the calling went on to contribute to their tribes in many other fundamental ways. There was even a small number of tribesmen who never understood the calling and, untrained, attempted to control the cosmic power and went insane, scratching out their own eyes from the manifestation of the chaos they saw.

Manhood trials and going off to camp in the bush was about courage. Each person must face the world and its evil sooner or later. Some men retreated; some men took hold and dug into the fight of life even in the face of death. Enduring the pains and struggles of the trials prepared one for the hardships and struggles of life. To make it back to the village safely, with the wisdom of one's experience, was a sign that one had become a man.

*****

My name is Kamau, and this is my brother Baaku. We are sons of the chief to one of the last remaining tribes of the earth that practice and live in the culture of the old ways. Years ago, our tribes have been pushed to the verge of extinction as result of the invading forces from Eurasia. Many survivors of the raids have fled to safety in the swamplands and jungle of the Sudd.

Our father is now preparing us for the annual initiation ceremony and manhood trials, which is a mystical and age-old tradition. Boys go into the swamps jungle, secluded and cut off from the tribe to survive on their own for five months in the bush. This will be a test of character in the face of adversity. Initiates have to collect materials to build a hut to live in, so father is identifying to Baaku and me the proper flexible saplings to cut and grass to dry for thatching. Every custom and preparation is detailed and complex, like the proper way to slaughter goats and cows, which hunting or tracking technique to use, and how to supply months' worth of food. The anxiety is by itself killing me from my excitement, let alone remembering the language and techniques of ceremonies and trials.

Father goes over the instructions with Baaku and me. He is adamant about us knowing the importance of these skills, and that, it is a matter of life or death with any situation in the bush.

"Baaku, Kamau, listen to me, sons," says Father. "The mind is a muscle, and you need to challenge it. If not, it becomes weak and will grow small. Never take matters of the mind lightly. Think of the universe and all its wonders. Man, compared to the universe, is but a portion to a larger whole, and the essence of man comes from the universe. The universe is limitless with no bounds. For one to master the spirit of self, one must allow for strength to come from within. From within, all wisdom and strength will come from within the universe without limit. Negative energies will always try to flank you and trick you, make you lose focus and cloud your judgment. But abandon pride and stay tough but gentle, strong but soft. Remember, your skills and abilities are not to impress or to boast. Stay pure and true to the positive vibrations, and nothing will be able to conquer you!"

"Yes, Father!" respond Baaku and Kamau. They can sense the emotion in their father's words. This will be the last time that we brothers will be together as boys or see any members of the village for the next five months. Many boys have lost their lives during the long, hard months, but it is a title of honor to go through the trials. Knowing the existing dangers we will face, we understand that suffering and pain represent the trials of life, and we face it with no fear.

With the crackling sounds of campfire wood burning, a group of boys with their heads bowed in submission, sit in a circle around a large campfire. Their bodies are smeared in an orange clay substance with the markings of the tribes. Male tribe elders sit in a half-circle in front of the boys, as they commence the opening ceremony of manhood trials.

"You have chosen to walk the path of courage and wisdom. You have chosen to put your spirits up against the path of the warrior-mystics. A journey into the very heart of the swamps jungle and darkness will challenge the heart and spirit of the initiates. You have inherited special abilities and even more latent talents to manifest," says the village elder. "But which type of man are you? Are you a man to fight evil in the face of death, or are you a man to retreat and give in to the wills of evil? Courage and sacrifice is the path to manhood, and the path to manhood is action, and through actions are which energies that will manifest. Which path of action will you choose— to stand in the name of justice with no surrender, or no retreat? Or does one get imprisoned and engulfed by the conditions of man? I bid you farewell on your trials of manhood, my young examples of bravery among men," closes the village elder.

Ceremonial drums begin to bang, and the male village elders from the tribe begin to sing in unison, while dancers wearing different masks that represent the spirits of different animals perform traditional dances. The speaker of the ceremony takes a sip from a ceremonial cup and then passes the cup around to the elders, next to the boys circled around the campfire signifying the passing of tradition through the generations. Next, the boys have the hairs of their bodies shaven, as this will be the last evening that the boys will be together as boys. Tonight, they will fill themselves with the best choices of goat and cow, enjoying that boyish laughter one last time, for in the morning, they will head off into the swamps to stand the trials of manhood.

For one last night, Kamau and Baaku spend their time together as boys with their friends from the village. They stand in a bunch laughing and making jokes.

"I still can't believe your little brother will be taking the trial tests at an earlier age than you, Baaku!" shouts one of the boys.

"No matter, Jela, we all have to make it through just the same, yourself included," responds Baaku. "He is my brother. He has had a good example to follow. I will stand with the title warrior-mystic, following the footsteps of my father in wearing the talisman of the tribes," states Baaku.

Unannounced, Kamau backs away from the group of boys and walks away, with Baaku soon following behind him.

"Kamau!" Baaku calls after his brother. "Worried about the trials, little brother?" he asks Kamau, him knowing his brother to be one to sit and think on things.

"You know me, brother. I am always off in my head thinking of the cosmos," says Kamau. "I cannot stop thinking on how I am going to miss the faces of Mother and Grandmother and the company of being around baby sister," Kamau says to his brother.

"Oh, brother, they will be fine while we are away. It is in our bloodline to be strong. We are destined for greatness, Kamau!" says Baaku, looking toward the stars. "Everything will be fine, Kamau. You will see."

The following morning at dawn, men at the camp rise and awaken the initiates, who are then blindfolded, while the men slowly dance, sing, and chant along the camp. There is an electric feeling in the atmosphere as an assortment of staff-like spears are being brandished by the men. The initiates are then guided to the edge of camp where the blindfolds are uncovered, and suddenly, the boys break out into a full sprint heading into the jungle, being chased by the men screaming and waving their spears. Hearts pounding out of their chests, the boys come to a point in the jungle where they come to find that an assistant has been strategically placed in the bush to help with the first process of building their huts and the second custom of circumcision. Initiates will build the home they are to live in for the next five months, while they wait for the appearance of the doctor to perform the foreskin removal procedure. The performer of foreskin removal is a distant cousin of one of the tribes that has studied various practices for the advancement of the tribes at the university in the city of Ethiopia. He is only allowed to appear to perform the procedure on the initiates.

*****

Kamau works diligently with his assistant gathering saplings and dry grass, keeping his focus as he pondered over his father's instructions. Each initiate has been charged with encircling his home with a symbolic barrier representing his clan. The sun beams down on Kamau as he toils to build his home, but nevertheless, life is full of adventure, and his heart is filled with love and generosity. After the completion of building Kamau's hut, he and his assistant come wandering to a stream not too far from where Kamau has set up camp, and they find a strange girl, who is not from any of the tribes, fetching water.

Kamau approaches the young girl, speaking with greetings and salutations, offering the girl help, but the girl does not respond to him. She does not even budge; she just ignores Kamau. The girl's lack of reply prompts Kamau to look strangely toward his assistant. He shrugs his shoulders, thinking that the girl must not have heard him.

Kamau moves closer to the girl. He stretches out his hand to tap her on the shoulder.

"Excuse me, are you lost? Can I, in anyway, assist you?" asks Kamau. Still, the girl gives no reply. Baffled by the girl's silence, Kamau turns his back on the girl and starts to walk away.

Not an instance later, the girl shudders and twists her head to reveal her face, and what the assistant witnesses as Kamau walks away from the girl is not a face of a girl but that of a snake—an Ethiopian python! The boys have heard stories of the vicious snake that killed boys by strangling them to death and eating them whole. With an ill-tempered ferocity, the snake quickly circles Kamau, stretching its long body. It has to be at least twenty feet long. Kamau looks like an easy prey for the constrictor's gullet. It flashes its rows of long, curved teeth that lined the python's flexible jaws, as it looks for the proper moment to lash out and strike Kamau. The eyes of the snake tell that it is going to strike Kamau, and it does.

Kamau goes without thinking; he makes a dive and rolls into the dirt. Then jumping to his feet, Kamau takes off in a dash in an attempt to get away from the snake's mandibles. As Kamau runs to reposition himself, the massive python swipes its tail, knocking over Kamau and making him stumble to the ground. Kamau panics, and he slips. While trying to regain his footing, the snake sees his target's mistake, and it strikes again. This time, the constrictor lands its teeth right in the shoulder of Kamau, making him wince and scream out in pain. The cries of Kamau as he struggles to battle the python has begun to sound like drowned-out gurgles, as the constrictor curls its body around Kamau, suffocating its victim.

Kamau jumps awake from his sleep inside of his hut screaming; he is drenched in sweat. Kamau looks around the hut; he figures he must have fallen asleep and started seeing visions in his sleep from the heat of the day. Kamau's assistant steps inside the entryway of the hut wielding his blade, ready to chop off the head of any attacking predator. He eyes Kamau and then scans the inside of the hut, checking to see that all is clear. He sees the sweat-drenched Kamau and says to him, "The elders say that the voices that you hear in your head and the visions that you see all mean something. It is time. The doctor is here," he informs. Kamau steps outside his hut to the sight of the surgeon waiting for him with his spear in hand.

Kamau sits on the bare ground of his hut, only draped in a blanket, as the doctor cleans and prepares for the procedure. As Kamau sits with his legs spread, the doctor in one swift cut removes the foreskin. Kamau makes no noise; he does not even flinch. His absolute bravery is the fundamental importance. His wounds are then dressed in a plant of medicinal substance and wrapped with a leather thong around his waist. Kamau makes no sound, as he sees glimpses of the fading sunlight marking the last day he would see as a boy. Kamau hears a voice speak to him as he dozes off into the night, "He who runs at night will fall many times!"

On the morning of the eleventh day of pain and discomfort, Kamau appears from his hut, crutched over a stick, barely able to stand. He has grown weak and lost weight, surviving the long days of eating corn grains and no water for the first eight days. His assistant is, a diamond in the rock, keeps wood on the fire during the long cold nights, as Kamau sleeps, recovering on his blanket. Kamau barely talks as he hobbles around the camp, fatigued and in pain. Today is the first day for Kamau to eat a much-needed full meal because within the next few days, after he regains his strength and energy, Kamau will be on his own for the next four months.

The days of recovery are slow for Kamau. He walks around the boundaries of his camp, chopping firewood, which he does not mind. This gives him time to communicate with his animal friends. Kamau has not made many friends with the boys of the tribe, but he has befriended many different animal companions that has kept him company. By day 30, Kamau's strength and energy has returned and his spirits are high. He begins to practice his stick-fighting form and hand-movement combinations, mastering his craft in mosquito-and-fly fist form. While Kamau is reflecting over his teacher's directions and remembering the whacks from his bamboo cane for punishment, he can hear his instructor. "Every victory is hard fought. A warrior-mystic is a true virtuoso who could adapt to many hand-to-hand combat and projectile skills."

Most of Kamau's time is spent over the next few months hunting waterfowl and small rabbits in the bush, fishing for river perch, perfecting his skills, or staying in meditation. On his spirit quest, Kamau has learned something every day from the land or his ancestors. He has learned that his hardships have only come from the land and that his people have had everything they needed—freshwater, wild animals to hunt, and livestock.

What else did they need with the outside world? thinks Kamau.

One evening around dusk, the winds are heavy, and the smell of precipitation in the atmosphere has indicated to Kamau that the clouds are full of rain and are ready to let loose. Kamau, losing track of the day in meditation and training, has forgotten to resupply his stock of firewood. After cooking, he will not have enough wood to keep his fire lit through the heavy storm. Therefore, Kamau has decided that he'd better take off into the bush to gather more firewood before the weather gets any worse.

Quickly Kamau works at chopping firewood before the rain begins to pour. Suddenly he gets an eerie feeling, as if he feels eyes watching him from behind a field of papyrus bush. The clouds start to roll with thunder, and flashing bolts of lightning illuminate the sky. Kamau swings his head to survey his surroundings. He recognizes a purring growl coming from straight ahead of him. Dead in front of him, Kamau notices the stalking golden orbs as their eyes meet.

A massive lion leaps from within the bush of reeds; its mane is full and unruly, as it rapidly gnashes its canines at Kamau. Following the large predator, two lions, a bit smaller than the first, pounces out of the bush—one standing at each of the alpha's side. Their manes have not yet fully come in. One of the smaller lions takes a step toward Kamau, eagerly glaring its teeth, but the larger male takes a swipe at the lion. The power from the strike knocks the smaller male back into its place. Imposing its size, the massive superior roars, making the other tuck its tail and cower in position.

Kamau begins to walk backward, slowly taking small steps, not making any sudden moves as he carefully paces himself. He keeps his eyes on the beast, crouched in position with his spear and machete in hand. Kamau prepares himself for battle, as he unexpectedly crosses paths with a pride of ravaging and ravenous lions. The predators with the look in their faces, staring as if they had been roaming for hours and were seeking food in anyway. Kamau, staring into the eyes of the massive alpha as it barred down on him, stands firm as he thinks in his head his best defensive strategy against his opponents. Then the beast speaks to him.

"Boy, who are you? What are you doing here? Shouldn't you be running?" inquires the lion in a deep, rumbling resonance that could compete with the overture of thunder.

"I am not afraid," says Kamau calmly. "And you're sadly mistaken, lion of the jungle. I am not a boy, but I am a warrior, and I live for combat!" says Kamau, making it well-known that he is prepared to fight.

"Ha, foolish little warrior! I have devoured the flesh and bones of many boys claiming to be great warriors, and the age has been of no matter. What chance of hope does the likes of you have against me, little warrior?" says the lion.

"I am Kamau, son of Tua, chief to the last of the earth tribes surviving in the motherland of Ethiopia, and I am ready to stand and fight!" yells Kamau at the beast.

The lion is amazed at the boy who had shown no fear, and he chuckles. "The chase would have made this encounter much more exciting, lest you have the honor of being a good meal before the storm, brave little warrior."

"I'd rather die than give the likes of you the pleasure of seeing my back," replies Kamau.

"Wretched human!" the lion snarls at the insult.

"Stay pure and true, fight to the death, and die with honor!" screams Kamau.

As the alpha leaps forward pouncing toward Kamau, they impact and make contact, and a spontaneous bolt of lightning strikes from the ground, sending the massive beast and Kamau flying in opposite directions. They both fall and hit the ground with a thud. The pair of male lackeys scurry back into the bush.

Kamau hits the ground, shuddering and shacking, then a stream of electricity flowing around his body suspends him into the air as if contained in a firmament. His eyes have lost its pupils, and they begin to glow an electric blue color. "Aaahhh!" Kamau lets out an agonizing yell of pain, releasing a giant surge of electricity. His body again drops to the ground, and the rain from the storm starts to fall.

"You have been chosen to walk the path of warrior-mystics. The balance of the universe is within…" a mythical utterance vibrates in the mind of Kamau, and a vision of various animal essences unveil themselves for the first time to the sight of the warrior-mystic.

The sound of birds chirping startle awake a sleeping Kamau, who now lays on his single-layered blanket on the floor of his hut with his eyes halfway open from the shinning sun. Attempting to recall the ending of the previous night, Kamau knows that he is not dead from the encounter with the pride of lions. The aching pain of his limbs will not let the notion be true. He can only clearly remember the happening of the storm, the massive size of the lion, and a fuzzy memory of the alpha male leaping to attack. His body is sore as if he went through the foreskin removal process again. Kamau observes that he has a wound across his chest that has been dressed. Slowly he shuffles to the entryway of his hut, and what his eyes see, Kamau cannot help but smile. In the past four months, Kamau has not seen or has had any contact with a person, family, or friend. Appearing from his hut, he sees the carcass of the massive alpha male that he had the encounter before. Standing behind the body of the beast are Kamau's trial assistant with a tribe elder, both expressing wide smiles. Both their presence is an indication that he has become a man and that it is time to return to the village and be crowned for homecoming.

*****

In a province submerged in chaos, located in the region of South Sudan, a newly crowned king sits in his council hall, pondering to himself on how to expand his empire in the motherland, which is filled with war and terror. The king thinks himself a god and envisioned a ferocious empire and kingdom that has mirrored his image. He aims to force everyone into man's religion or force them to flee the country, claiming that the future will be his. The tyrant disregards old treaties and honors no contracts. His method to grow his powers is by any means. The doors of the hall room flies open, and in comes running one of the king's personal guards.

"My lord, we have someone with information. They are inquiring about the reward in the marketplace." The news arouses the king's attention.

"Bring him in," commands the king.

Abandoning all his hopes in the old ways of the tribe, he is all about advancement and power. Sick and disgusted with the reminiscent of the arcane ruins, Isingoma, whose father had been banished from the earth tribes by the present chief's father for practicing methods of medical experimentation that went against the ways of the tribe. Isingoma's father refuse to stop his work in progressing methods, resulting in the exile of his family from within the tribes, but the father and his son are bound by a curse to return to the tribes every year to perform ceremonial procedures. Isingoma is bent on revenge on the tribes and on avenging his family name for the humiliation they had suffered. He feels that the tribes have lacked respect for his intellect and his family. Isingoma is more than ready to sacrifice the lives of his tribesmen to appease the new king in power and be in his good graces.

"Ah, Doctor!" says the king, greeting Isingoma with a big smile and his arms open. "What good news do you bring your king? Tell me the secrets of this tribe in the swamps so that they will be mine!" says the king.

Isingoma informs the king many of the tribe's secrets, exposing his knowledge of the bond and its fundamental theory. The doctor also tells the king of how secretive the tribes' people are and that they have various safeguards in place as protection barriers.

"So, Doctor, how do you suppose the best way to mount an attack on the tribes?" asks the king.

Isingoma allows the king in on his plan to use one of the chief's son, whom he has established a good relationship over the years. The boy has visions of being a part of the modern world. So they figure they can use this to their advantage. Isingoma gives the king information on the tribes' manhood trials, informing him that the boy should be off alone in the bush.

The king orders his servants to prepare some of his best foods and materials, showering Isingoma in rewards. The next day, the king sends Isingoma, escorted by four of his best guards, back into the swamps of the Sudd to visit and talk with the boy.

*****

Wearing crowns of palm leaves atop of their freshly shaven heads, the initiates who had left the tribe village five months earlier as boys, have now returned to their homes as men. Male tribe elders and future initiates lead the processions back into the village. Banners of the tribes are flapped by the gales of wind, and drums are banged. Initiates and elders participate in song and dance. Before they cross the village threshold, they form a single line as they move through the village. Women sing and shout for their sons' return. Some fall to the ground in tears of joy, knowing that a lot of boys in the past did not make it back home from their trials. But this season, all of them have returned, even though some exhibited injury. All this season's boys have returned as men of the tribe. Small children fall in line, joining in on the celebration.

The initiates are led into the village circle of ceremony, where they are greeted by their families and friends, whom they have not seen in months. Initiates and family members trade stories and accounts of their past months' experiences. Most of all, spirits are high in the village. The initiates are now men in the eyes' of the tribe, but not all are called to walk the path of the warrior-mystics. In fact, there is only one in this season's group of boys that has received a call from the ancestors, and that has ruffled a few feathers.

There is an odd feeling in the air that Kamau can sense from his brother. Baaku, the quintessential tough guy, has not been acting so tough. He has been upset about not receiving a call to the path of warrior-mystics, but his little brother Kamau has. Kamau just hopes that Baaku does not feel so hard on himself and feel as if he still is not a great warrior.

"Hey, Baaku," says Kamau to his brother, who is being a little bit standoffish and to himself. "Still upset about not getting a calling?" asks Kamau, knowing Baaku has to be in a funk about his childhood dream being unraveled.

"Now I know what it feels like to be squashed flatter than a dung beetle," responds Baaku somberly. "I have always dreamed of the day that I would receive the calling to the path of warrior-mystics and follow the footsteps of father and grandfather and lead the tribesmen, bearing the talisman of power. But you were always there, always on my trail, always keeping pace with me, and most times beating me. I never wanted to think it, or admit it. I just thought we were in great competition to push each other, doing what brothers do. I tried my best to take the lead, but as we got older, in those moments of hurt, anger, and guilt for letting my younger brother defeat me. I tried to open up to the fact that you just may be better than me. I attempted to accept the thought and gather strength from it, but in the end, bitterness and darkness cloud my heart. I am a fool, Kamau. I just do not know how to show my face in the village without walking the path of warrior-mystics," says Baaku.

"There are many great things you can still accomplish. You are still a great warrior, Baaku. Like you said before, it is there in our bloodline and heritage. Think of grandfather. His calling came late, but he still became a great warrior and leader preceding that," professes Kamau.

"A late calling—that is no guarantee in having the honor of walking the path of warrior-mystics, Kamau!" responds Baaku.

"Do not get to down on yourself, Baaku. There is time. We have lots of great things to do together. One thing about it is that I will always be your little brother and will always look up to you!" says Kamau, throwing his arm around Baaku's shoulder, attempting to uplift his brother's spirit. "Now stop with the bad energy and let's go enjoy our time with the family," says Kamau. "I am really looking forward to spending time with baby sister and hearing what Grandmother has been up to while we were away."

The families of the tribe spend the remainder of the evening enjoying one another's company around the large bonfire. Families have stuffed their bellies with spoonsful of corn grains and meats. The male village elders and tribe members sit from old to young in succession of the generations telling stories and giving speeches while they sip cups of fermented yeast and berries. The village is full of joy and laughter, which rings out into the late hours of the night, as the people of the earth tribe celebrated the passing of the ages.

The following morning, just before the sun breaks the sky's horizon at dusk, during the stint, members of the village sleep in the warmth and comfort of their loved ones, their bellies full of food and wine. Their children, exhausted from a night of dancing and playing, lay resting, having dreams of the beautiful times to come in the future and this morning's grand breakfast.

*****

The sound of footsteps treading through water is heard as a restless member of the tribe anxiously wades through a stream that boarders the village. He reaches a certain point and starts to maneuver his hands in a certain motion, and then he utters the word *release!* Instantly, there is a wailing groan that resonates through the mist and trees of the swamp. The tribesmen continues to his planned meeting location.

"Isingoma!" he whispers, looking around. "Isingoma, are you here?" he asks, projecting the volume of his voice just above a whisper.

"Young Baaku, how nice to see you here as planned," says Isingoma, appearing from behind a bush of reeds.

A battalion of soldiers positioned along the swamps' edge sits, waiting for their commander's signal to advance.

"Do you really think people live in there?" a solider speaks, staring into the mists of the Sudd.

"With the mosquitoes and flies the size of our horses, if people do live in there, they must be a breed of beasts and savages who must be destroyed before they run amok!" responds the other soldier.

Moments later, the soldiers' battalion leader approaches. "We have been given the orders to move into position by General Chimola," says the squad captain.

*****

"Beware of the prodigal son that returns home!" a mythical voice vibrates. Along with a blaze of fire, followed by yells of people screaming in pain, the grim premonition stirs a sleeping grandmother from her sleep, making her jump awake and clench her chest.

*****

Sniff! Isingoma takes in a deep inhale of morning air, as he strolls through the village entry, which he used to call his home long ago as a little boy, before his father and family were banished from the village. But this morning, Isingoma returns home with a homecoming present that will shape the future of the tribes and the future world as we know it.

A tribe security member walks his perimeter as he takes heed to the presence of the tribe's ceremonial doctor.

"Your tasks at the ceremonies are complete, Isingoma. Why are you here?" shouts the on-post guard, catching Isingoma's attention.

"Oh, just inviting myself to morning breakfast. I have a dish that I have been just dying to serve," replies Isingoma to the guard.

Speechless to Isingoma's statement, the guard then notices a line of torches moving from beyond the bush. "Someone has released the barrier!" cries the tribe solider to himself. The guard glances at Isingoma and breaks into a sprint to alarm the people that war has come to the village. Drums and horns of war blare through the village, and the chief rushes to the front lines to defend his people.

"Chief Tua!" speaks Isingoma to the tribe leader.

"Doctor, what are you doing here?" demands the chief.

"The days of the tribes are over, Tua!" screams Isingoma. "Your time is over. The secrets of the earth tribes' true power has been with you for too long, and it is time for me to claim it!" says Isingoma. "Never have I or never will I have mercy for the likes of you!" spats the doctor.

"If that is what you feel, Isingoma, come take it!" replies Chief Tua.

"Putting up a fight, of course, but it is of no matter. There is no escape. Your efforts are futile!" says Isingoma.

"Treasures will get spent, and glory will fade, Isingoma, but justice and honor will endure forever. I am not afraid of you, and I am not afraid of death!" decrees Chief Tua.

"I expected nothing of the less!" replies Isingoma, and with those words, a band of arrows cover the morning sky, engulfing what is left of the sight of the sun.

It is as if time has stopped. The village is in chaos. Homes fall to shambles as they burn. Children cry as they run aimlessly. Women scream and yell while warriors of the tribe mount their best defenses from the unexpected attack. Kamau runs among the anarchy and fights his way toward the front of the village to help defend against the overrunning hordes of invading soldiers. Making his way to the battlefront, Kamau witnesses his brother, Baaku, running in the opposite direction of the attack. Kamau gives chase after his brother.

"Baaku! Baaku!" yells Kamau, drawing his brother's attention. "Baaku, where are you going?" asks Kamau hysterically. "We have to find Mother and Grandmother!" states Kamau.

Baaku, the firstborn son of the chief to the tribes' people and older brother of Kamau, can hardly look his brother in the eyes. Baaku has half the mind to not stop and just keep running away from his brother. Kamau can sense that Baaku is running from another turmoil, which has nothing to do with helping the front lines.

"Baaku, what's wrong? What have you done?" asks Kamau.

Baaku pauses for a moment and turns to look at his brother. "I only wanted to intimidate you and the others. I felt that you were taking away my position in the tribe. I trusted him when he said he wanted to help the tribes, but he lied, and I did not know this would happen!" responds Baaku.

"He who? What are you talking about, Baaku?" inquires Kamau, perplexed by what Baaku is saying.

"Isingoma, the doctor," replies Baaku, and without another word, he turns and runs in his cowardice.

"Our homes are being destroyed. It is inevitable. Nothing last forever. We must rebuild what has been destroyed. The hate and greed of our brothers have destroyed our refuge!" wails one of the village elders as the homes of his people are being burned.

Warriors of the tribe, men and women, husbands and wives stood side by side battling to defend their homes and salvage what is left of their ancient culture. For every invading soldier that the warriors of the tribes put on their backs and eliminated, three more spawn and jump into the fight. Waves on top of waves, the battalions of soldiers continue to pour into the village. And with every essences of their beings, the tribemen fought on in what seemed like a feeble attempt at survival. Corned by a squadron of soldiers and displaying the bravest actions of character, Kamau and his family stood side by side, without Baaku, fighting in the battle for their homes and prevention of the extinction of their culture. Even though it is clear that the village has been overrun by the sheer number of invading soldiers and they stand no real chance at winning the battle, they fight.

"Kamau, where is your brother?" asks the mother of Kamau as she held his baby sister in her arms, shielding her in a barrier of protection.

"I don't know where Baaku is!" shouts Kamau as he fends off two attacking soldiers. "The last I seen of Baaku, he was running away from the front lines of the village, just before I found you and Grandmother. Baaku had done something foolish. He was saying something about Isingoma, but he said no more before he continued to flee," explains Kamau. The news of her firstborn son's absence nearly brings Kamau's mother to collapse, resulting in a break of her concentration, causing the surrounding barrier to flicker.

"No matter the news of Baaku at this present time, Bahati," says the grandmother of Kamau, taking the hand of her daughter, "we must keep our strength and focus. All good fortune has not left us yet!" says the former elder tribe leader and warrior now old in her age.

"Yes, Mother Amina, I understand," replies Bahati. "It's just my heart that breaks with pain," she states.

"It is all our hearts that breaks at the missing presence of Baaku, but we must stay committed to taking out as many soldiers as possible and guiding the children to safety," says Grandmother Amina. "But young Baaku will have to pay for his betrayal toward the tribes. The cosmos will not allow the essences of his spirit to rest until he rights the wrongs that he has caused here today!" decrees the elder.

After putting up one hell of a fight defending the village against a barrage of arrows, Chief Tua is badly wounded and overwhelmed by the attack. Looking in the face of the destruction of the tribe's village, the great warrior is challenged with the decision no parent wishes to be forced to make. He knows within himself, no matter how unjust it maybe, but for the survival of the tribe's lineage and future, they have to separate from their children so that they could make an escape, if there is any chance for the survival of the tribes. Chief Tua glances toward his wife and his mother with tears in his eyes.

Having the grasp of the magnitude of the situation, both women burst into controllable sobs. They do not even need to express the words. Grandmother Amina has been raising her son to live for moments as such as these since he was a little boy, her reminiscing on her time as a child fleeing her home village. She tightly embraces her son for one last time, grasping his face in the palm of her hands and pausing with a deep gaze into his eye's, then she places a kiss on Chief Tua's cheek, turning away from her son.

"Bahati," says Chief Tua, calling to his wife. "It is time. I cannot hold back the battalions much longer," he says to his wife, taking her hand within his, as his wife hysterically wails. "We shall be forever together in the cosmos. Our love is written in the stars, so we will always be eternal in the cosmos, Bahati!" he says to his wife in an impossible attempt to lighten her spirit of the burden.

"Kamau, you must take your sister and leave for your safety!" says Chief Tua to his second-eldest son. "The village has been over-taken, and there is not much hope for victory at this point. We are completely unprepared for the numbers in this attack," he explains. "You will be the lasts of the earth tribes of the motherland and what remaining culture that has not yet been all driven to extinction. You will have to carry on the ways of our people for the good of our future lineage and tribe. Always remember that you are of the earth and exist within the universe. You must go and be proud of the tribe, pro-tect your sister, and show her our ways!" says Chief Tua to Kamau; he then removes the ancient necklace and medallion of the tribes from around his neck. "Take this," he says, handing his son the talisman.

"The talisman of power!" utters Kamau, in shocked astonishment.

"The talisman of power holds the secrets and powers of the tribes. You must always protect it and keep it safe. Don't forget, my children. I love you, and you must grow up to be a strong warrior," says the Chief to his son, who refused to leave the side of his father during battle. But Chief Tua stresses the importance of Kamau's and his sister's escape to his strong-willed son. "We cannot waste time," commands Chief Tua. The father expresses his affection to his children one last time, just before he makes one last courageous move. With the last of his strength, Chief Tua straighten his posture, standing in the tribes' ancient fighting form. The ancient markings of the tribes that lined the chief's body began to glow, and his feet begin to fuse with the earth. He then motions his hands as if he were pressing down toward the earth. "Go now! This is your opportunity," commands the chief to his family, and simultaneously he raises his right foot, along with about five yards of dirt, and stomps down within the earth, creating a massive crack into the earth that had crated and winding fissure, engulfing a squad of soldiers. "Go!" he screams, throwing himself on course to create another distraction so that his family can make a getaway.

With no time to waste, both Bahati and Grandmother Amina cautiously traverse across what just stood hours ago as their tribes' home and refuge, now devastated by the betrayal and revenge of a tribesman's plot, which resulted in their way of life being reduced to ashes and piles of cinder. Grandmother Amina in her age tries her best to keep pace with the swift and agile young Kamau, as he holds tight her hand as they make their escape. But witnessing the ravage of the village, along with the sight of burning huts and bodies, the burden of pain and sorrow weighed on her heart. Grandmother Amina's empathic senses kick into overdrive. She feels a shortness of breath; she staggers and collapses to the ground.

Kamau, alarmed by the abrupt stop in movement, can feel the heaviness in his grandmother's body. "Grandmother Amina!" calls Kamau, rushing to aid his grandmother in rising from the ground. "Are you OK?" he asks earnestly to his grandmother.

"Baby, I am fine, just fine. These old bones are just a bit tired from all the activity. This body of mine is not as limber as it was in the old days," responds Grandmother Amina. "There is no time to lose. We must keep moving," she says. Grandmother Amina dusts herself off, while being escorted from the ground by Kamau.

As they regroup to continue on to their pathway, Bahati doubles back to check on the fallen mother of her husband and grandmother to her son Kamau, making sure that all is well with the party. "We must hurry. The secret pathway out of the village is just up ahead," says Bahati. Just as the family proceeds to continue in their march, a unit of soldiers catches sight of the family's position and makes a rapid approach.

"*Waaaa!*" cries the baby sister of Kamau. With her glaring eyes, she brings notice of the advancing troops to the anxious group.

"We must move now," says Kamau assertively.

"No matter how fast we move now, we will never get away from the soldiers with these old legs," says Grandmother Amina, taking a firm grip to her walking staff.

"What are you talking about?" inquires a frantic Kamau to the words of his grandmother.

"My child, I have had my time on this earth, and now it is time to return home," she says.

"No, Grandmother. What are you thinking about doing? You cannot. There is still time. We can still make it," expresses Kamau to his grandmother.

"Oh, baby, you do not have to worry. My purpose is my purpose, and the time to act in that purpose is now. It is an honor to give my life so that you can live to give your life so that she can live," says Grandmother Amina, embracing Kamau and taking hold of his baby sister.

Kamau can no longer hold back his tears as the reality of his world has come crashing down upon him in ruins.

"Listen, young warrior," his grandmother says to him, "you must be strong so that you can live. All that has happened here today cannot be in vain. The continuity of our future lives within you, Kamau. You must always remember that true energy is never destroyed. It's only transferred, and that we are of the universe, so therefore forever bonded in the cosmos," explains Grandmother Amina to Kamau.

"You always liked my stories most," she says to a sobbing Kamau, who is trying his best to muster his resolve. "Pick your head up. Be proud, baby, always be proud. I love you! Now go. Do not worry. I have a few tricks left up my sleeves!" Grandmother Amina winks at Kamau and gives both her grandchildren large hugs and kisses before they continue their advance.

"I am a lot older from the days when I was a fiery young girl and yearned for combat and battle. But today's occurrence has deeply saddened me. I must admit I had thought that my eyes had seen the last of war and destruction of this magnitude years ago," utters the elder to herself, as she watches the approach of the invading unit. "I have always wanted so much more out of life than what man's new society has to offer in its dominating and abusive ways. My faith is deeply rooted in the essence of the earth and universe. I completely understand that by no means are we perfect creatures. This called purpose of my heart is to set blaze a trail of inspiration, lead the charge in keeping the family together, and instill in the children to make the most out of the best essences of themselves," says Grandmother Amina. Expressing still in her age that when it comes to her love for her family and tribes, it is as solid as a rock. "Down this rapid trek of destruction, there will be nothing left of man's true potential in the future. Events and stories of their past, such as this, will set the ripples of division and hate across the generations. The spirit of the tribes must remain. Our strength and redemption rests eternally in the cosmos," says the elder.

Grandmother Amina takes in the ambience of the village one last time, as she prepares herself to make an unforgettable sacrifice. She breathes easy as she makes peace with her final decision, knowing that she will most likely die from the energy exerted during the process. Tears fell from the eyes of the elder, as she displays the agony of the pain she feels. Suddenly an uncontrollable array of green illumination shoots out of the mouth and eyes of the elder. "Aaaiiieeee!" she screams as her body lifts into the air, sending a swirling vortex of wind toward the soldiers, knocking some back to the ground and sending others flying off in small gusts. The exhibition comes to a sudden conclusion with a loud *wooosshh* and then *banng*; the body of

Grandmother Amina spontaneously combusts and disperses into tiny light particles that float in the sky. The particles form Grandmother Amina's countenance within the air shining a golden light before plummeting down into the earth, which instantly begins to transform the ground that has only borne dirt into a widening crevice where a tree has started to grow, expanding its size at a fast rate. The large tree obscures the soldiers' clear path in catching up to the elder's family as they flee the village, making her sacrifice in causing a distraction all the more valued.

Just before crossing outside the borderlines of the village, a devoted and caring Bahati and her children run into their next challenge to escape from their burning village into the bush and from the attacking soldiers. As the three proceed, they come across the gruesome sight of an invading unit that had been finding amusement in their work of impaling the bodies of their fellow tribesmen along the village edge, which had fallen during battle. The mother, knowing now more than ever, is the time for her to use her wits to protect her children from the pack of wild dogs attacking their village. Bahati settles in her mind the thought that she would rather die than to have the fate of her children's lives and destinies fall in the hands of the beastly invaders. It would be a mother's honor to die and give her life, making that sacrifice so that her children have a chance to go on and live.

"It is time, my son. You must take your sister and go," Bahati says to her son.

Kamau makes a meager gesture of defying the words of his mother, thinking he can never leave her side in such a critical time.

"The culture and the story of our people must live on, Kamau!" she says to her son. "The loss of human spirit's innocence at the expense of an ill-fated dream, warring between brothers and sisters, of which effects will be far-reaching well into the future, weakens the human bond between the earth and universe. Only the beauty and wonders of life can destroy such hate. Do not give in to the negative energies that lead to hate because as long as there is one to possess the talisman of power—one who stands with true pride and positive energy in the name of the tribes and clans born of the earth, children of Father Universe and Mother Earth—there is forever hope for the tribes in the cosmos!" says Bahati to her son, again displaying the stoutness of her character to stand alone in diverting the soldiers' attentions away from potentially capturing and killing her children. The painful moment is inevitable; the young warrior and baby sister have to make a move now if they are to have any chance of making it out of the village unnoticed. In the last seconds that Kamau and his mother would be together, he looks into the eyes of his mother. "I am so sorry this had to happen this way, my son," says Bahati, rubbing the head of her second-eldest son. "I love you, son! I love you, daughter!" she says before kissing the foreheads of her children. "Kamau, count twenty heartbeats and head in that direction," she directs Kamau, pointing in the opposite direction from the soldiers' position. Then she turns to run up ahead in pursuit of the unit.

"This ends now," says Bahati moments later on top of the soldiers' position. The first lady of the tribes stands prepared and strong, in her final offensive effort that will allow her children to escape from the invading army. "How dare you treat my fellow tribesmen with such disregard of respect?" she says to the unit, making her presence known. The unit of soldiers is baffled at the woman's presence and by her stance. The woman has made it clearly aware to the soldiers that she comes prepared, with no limits to how far she will go to protect her children.

"Ha, woman, what do you expect to do?" spits one of the unit soldiers in mockery of the woman's threat of attack.

"I guess we are just about to see about that," replies Bahati. Then she lets out a loud howl of ancient battle cries of the tribes and charges head on toward the group soldiers.

Twenty-five heartbeats after the instructed commands of his mother, Kamau stands with his sister in a trance, wailing her title as he holds is sister. Kamau knows life will never be the same, not long ago losing his entire family and village, just a day into his manhood. He snaps back into reality, heeding his mother's instructions to proceed in the other direction. As the siblings run away from their village, Kamau can hear the raging yells of his mother, and then a brilliant flash of magenta illuminates from beyond the wall of bushes and trees. The feeling is surreal to Kamau, as he and his baby sister run back into the bushes; he has just returned home from spending five months surviving there. But now he would return to the swamps and jungles of the Sudd as the sole provider, caretaker, and protector of his baby sister.

*****

The audible voice of Father Universe cast across the vastness of space, as he sets his gaze upon the events of the human from afar. "I have miscalculated miserably. First, as a father allowing the children of earth to attain the abundance of freewill too soon. Second, as a partner, failing to make clear the duties of the involved relationship. Ages ago, this rift has created the two opposing entities of positive and negative energy. Now thousands of millennia later, we stand here, staring at each other from across the voids and valleys of our points of views, perspectives, or what have you. The two energies' agents in opposition are at full force. The negative energies are in constant work in its attempt to overthrow the cosmic balance, while its counterbalance purpose is to keep it in line with the balance. Their messages are getting drowned in the echoes of foreign languages of hate and misunderstandings, to be forever lost in the reverberations of the voids," says Father Universe.

"The creatures of earth must remember that they are spirits of the cosmos and that power given and taken by force is nothing. So what do beings of the cosmos need with things in the nature of greed, lust, and hate? Humans' quest for its lost humanity will first begin with the freeing of the mind from the bondage of hate. But as long as there stands one in existence in the world that has not gone blinded with hate and greed, with pure energy in the face of evil, there will remain a small hope for a more humane world in the future and possibility to reunite the unbroken powers of the tribes."

CHAPTER 10

"I DON'T KNOW WHAT I am getting us into, Iesha," says Ronin. "All I know is that I have to see it through to make sure that Paul doesn't get hurt," says Ronin, as he sits in his bedroom in conversation with his younger sister, just before they prepare themselves for a night of events. This night will definitely lead the siblings on an epic journey of suspense and discovery. A natural at keeping his eyes and ears to the streets, Ronin feels that he can investigate the details of the situation from an inside angle better than any detective can. With the loss of one of his best friends, his insides will not sit right with him. He has to find out some solid information or reveal some type of evidence, and the information of the meeting that his friend PG gave him is a perfect place to start. Ronin knows how dangerous this can be, but he has made it his mission to infiltrate the street-gang's operation to gain as much information to clear PG of any wrongdoing, expose the gang's operation, and identify the killer of his friend. But first, he has to be sure not to blow his cover and get PG and himself killed during his investigation.

"You just make sure you don't get yourself killed during the process, Ronin!" snaps Iesha at her brother, expressing her uneasy feelings about Ronin's plan to go undercover. "What if the guy is there? What if he shows up and just blows your whole plan up from the start?" questions Iesha.

"With all the news and police activity, I highly doubt it that this dude will be out and about the next day with his face out in the open," states Ronin. "That's not how this type of guy thinks. He will want to be somewhere, lay low, and hide. He will be somewhere where he is surrounded by trusted people. He knows that they will not talk if they know anything. And guys like that, guys that work in the streets, they usually have lots of cash on hand, along with the contacts to access a network that they can be right next door, and we will not even know it until they want us too!" explains Ronin to Iesha.

"As always, Ronin, you make a damn good argument! Sounds damn good, and sounds like you know a hell of a lot more about this type of stuff than I do. But like I said, just don't get yourself killed during the process. Ma will be hysterical, and then I will have to find a way to bring you back from the dead and kill you again myself!" says Iesha to Ronin. Then Iesha picks herself from the side of her brother's bed and lays her hand on top of Ronin's crown. "I have to go shower. It's almost time to go!" she says to Ronin and heads out of the room, closing the bedroom door behind her.

*****

Just as the sun descends behind the horizon of the city of Providencia Beach, Detective Toussaint cruises the streets of the city. He carefully plans his strategy to follow up on the lead on the tips of two potential suspects. Detective Toussaint has received his information from a couple of ladies of the night whom he had associated himself with when he was working his beat on the street as a rookie. The street walkers are Detective Toussaint's ace in the hole for information when he needs to find out about a situation, and the detective is determined to find the street punk who murdered two innocent teenagers in cold blood.

But Detective Toussaint will soon find out that his time as lead detective of a special homicide unit, assembled from cross-county departments to investigate the cases that maybe linked to the same murder suspect, will be an arduous journey. Stressful time as it maybe to solve two murder cases on an ordinary day, the detective will learn shortly that running the gauntlet to attempt to hold the reins together among members of the investigating unit, which are divided between two divisional departments, will be more than a challenge that he has not come prepared for, and his life is about to take a turn down a nightmarish road. Detective Toussaint will soon be running through an obstacle course equipped with a grimy network of corrupt cops who see no problem with the old-school bribe or bullet culture. He will witness the actions of those who took a piece from whatever moved through the county lines, but at this time, Detective Toussaint is still enthusiastic and eager to solve the case. The detective is unaware of the type of game he has just signed himself up to play. He soon will find out that when he comes prepared to play a round of checkers, his oppositions are in a different league of their own, playing in a game of poker or a tournament of chess. Detective Toussaint rides into the city looking to prepare himself to solve the biggest case in his career, but little does he know of the world-breaking mysteries his life is getting ready to encounter as he rides into the fading light of the city.

*****

The mother of Ronin and Iesha's, Keisha's, stress level is beyond the point of exploding through the roof. This evening is the opening night of a new exhibit that she has been supervising and working on for the past nine months. On top of that is the nerve-wrecking worry that she has been experiencing for her son, who had just suffered the loss of a good friend and teammate just a day ago. And the shooter is still at large. Keisha is not sure if her son's life is also in danger, being that Ronin saw the face of the potential shooter. It really does not help her heart when Ronin came into her room to ask her if it was OK if he went over to his teammate and friend Paul's house. Keisha is just about to fall out, but she knows Ronin is grieving, and even though she wants to keep him quarantined inside the house, Keisha can't hold him in the house while she is gone for the night, and she'd rather not have Ronin in the house alone or by himself tonight. Therefore, she has agreed to get dressed a little earlier to drop Ronin off at Paul's place, just before she and Iesha head to the event at the museum.

Ronin rides in the back seat of his mother's car in contemplation of the coming hours ahead and his next moves. He attempts to completely humble himself and to clear his mind, thinking on the advantages and disadvantages of his position, hoping to prepare himself mentally, physically, and spiritually by taking on such a dangerous task. Ronin understands the culture and nature of street guys. He has had plenty of family experiences and history in the street life. He knows the basic social dos and don'ts, street terms, and phrases, so Ronin feels that he is not a complete square and will not look like a fish out of water. But Ronin does understand very well also that each gang or group has their various social orders or different ways of handling and dealing in business. Therefore, he will have to be patient in a sense, learn as much as possible, and be receptive of his surrounding influences in his environment. Ronin has also been eager to have another run-in with the mysterious older gentleman that he met the day previous. He knows there is no coincidence that he encountered the man and that he had to find him again because if anyone had answers to what was going on with Iesha and himself, it would be him.

Iesha is riding shotgun in the car in silence, but her head is speeding at a mile a minute trying to suppress the thoughts of her brother, Ronin, playing hero and putting his life at risk. Even though she thinks he is being reckless and should stay out of the way for the police, she knows how upset Ronin will be with her if she blows a whistle and alarm their mom of his plan. That will infuriate Ronin, and she has to admit it to herself that there is something strange happening with her and her brother. Iesha is just as anxious as Ronin is to find out what is going on with them. She can definitely agree with her older brother and not deny that they are dealing with some type of supernatural experience that no one living in the norms of ordinary society can explain this situation to the siblings.

All in all, thinks Iesha, *even though we may bicker and fight, annoy each other to the point to where we want to strangle each other, I love my brother to death, and I will not have life any other way.*

Her following behind Ronin's trail from sunup to sundown on his wild and crazy adventures allows the two to push each other in competition and to get the most out of one another. Their bond is unbreakable. They have more than the average brother-and-sister relationship, and she just wants him to know that she loves him to death, and she will do anything in the world for him to keep him alive.

ABOUT THE AUTHOR

As a collective species, most go throughout life looking to seek what they can gain and possess of the material world. At one point, I was a monster within myself, trapped under the obscured visions, clinging on to the memories of what life had told me to be. All the while, I was speeding into the walls of self-destruction as my humanity was consumed by the fires of society until I was able to face the monster in the mirror and ascend beyond the domain of my physical form and journey into the deepest parts of my character, therefore, find the truest essence of my spirit. I realized I only ever wanted to give something back to the world and become an everlasting beacon of inspiration and empowerment.

—Markee Drummer

THE FIRSTBORN SON TO MESHIA Miller and Jeffery Drummer, Markee arrived in the world from the cosmos on July 31, 1987, at St. Mary's Hospital in West Palm Beach, Florida.

It started as an idea, and those ideas turned into visions, which led him to action. Markee always knew that he would like to own or operate a business, not once had he thought of himself as an artist or author of anything. He still did not consider it now. Markee was in a nomadic state, clouded on his path of direction, just surviving. He had to find himself a way to express the thinking process in which he was going through. For many nights, he stared into the abyss of life pondering on which actions to partake in, reflecting on himself, character, and purpose. As his outlook grew, Markee began to see life, as being a continuous event of transiting energies—positive versus negative, good versus evil. Markee had decided, after a complete overview and understanding of the elements of his character, that it has always been and will always be Markee's duty to be a man of virtue. Markee homed in on himself and what it was that he could do on his own merits to bring peace within himself. No matter the cost, Markee had to perfect his character and craft, no matter what vices or follies he had to cross. Markee's benevolence must stand firm and true to his very end. So this project was started, as Markee's point of view of life's journey, using empirical knowledge and life encounters experienced by the author and those involved in his upbringing coming from an embellished perspective.

CPSIA information can be obtained
at www.ICGtesting.com
Printed in the USA
LVHW022003140821
695337LV00003B/345